Second Chance At The Riverview Inn

MOLLY O'KEEFE

MOLLY

O'KEEFE

Second Chance at the
RIVERVIEW INN

"You okay?"

"Totally," she lied. "You?"

He smiled.

Helen had seen some things. Some beautiful things. But, good lord forgive her, her child's first smile was NOTHING on Micah Sullivan's grin. It was so beautiful it robbed her of brain cells.

"I thought the closet was a bathroom," she said.

"You're not using it as a bathroom, are you?"

"No!" she said. "Just...taking a second."

She wasn't ready to get out of the closet, but clearly the time had come.

"I'm Helen," she said.

"Micah."

She laughed. "I know."

"Micah?" Jo's voice came around the bend of the hallway.

"I think that's our cue," Helen said and stepped around the bucket to get out of the closet, but to her surprise, Micah stepped in and shut the door behind him.

"You're not...*you're* not using it as a bathroom, are you?" she asked. And then wanted to die. *You just asked Micah Sullivan if he was going to pee in a closet.*

For all of you readers who have been so patient and have loved the Riverview Inn as much as I have. Thank you.

The Riverview Inn series is a series of standalone interconnected books. If this is your first visit to the Riverview check out the other books in the series!

Wedding At The Riverview Inn
Secrets At The Riverview Inn
Home To The Riverview Inn
Christmas At The Riverview Inn

CHAPTER
One

"I'M FINE," Helen said.

"Totally fine," her mom, Daphne, echoed.

They stood in the kitchen of the Athens Organics farmhouse, a bright yellow room with faded wooden floors and breakfast dishes in the sink. The kitchen Helen had grown up in. The safest place in the world.

"And if I become...not fine?" Helen asked. There were so many ways the situation she was walking into could become not fine. A whole spectrum of socially horrifying moments ranging from vomit and spontaneous combustion to, and it seemed completely possible and painfully likely, bursting into tears.

Mom stroked Helen's back like she was ten and home from school with a stomachache. It was comforting, if not weird, since she was twenty-nine. "Just find a cool dark place, gather your thoughts and you'll be—"

"Fine." Helen nodded.

She'd be fine because the worst had already happened to Helen. It was a law of averages kind of thing. Her fiance being killed in a car accident four years ago when Helen was five months pregnant had to insulate her against further disaster, right?

God. If only the world worked like that.

Helen took a deep breath, in through her nose, out through her mouth. *Crap. Was that right?* She tried it the other way, in through her mouth, out through her nose. And then back the other way.

I'm getting lightheaded.

"Honey," Mom said, the tone changing. Her mother was about to enable Helen putting on sweatpants and curling up with Bea to watch *Encanto* for the hundredth time. And she did not need to be enabled in that direction. She was doing this huge (but not really huge) thing. It was happening.

"Don't honey, me," Helen said, standing up straight and turning away from her mom to look at herself in the hall mirror. "I'm fine. We established that."

Any other person in her shoes would be ecstatic. Over the moon. And she was. She was also just really nervous.

She was going to meet her favorite rock group—Band of Outlaws. And her favorite singer—Micah Sullivan. Just thinking his name made her insides gooey and her brain whirr. She loved his voice and his songs, and in a few hours she would be looking right at his face. His in-person face. His super-hot, kind of snarling, kind of smiling face with the scar along his forehead from a bar fight in his misspent youth, and his blue, blue sex eyes.

It was a lot.

"How do I look?" Helen asked, turning to face her mom. "Should I change?" Again.

"You look perfect," Mom said. Which, well, was a standard Mom answer.

"Am I too casual?" Helen thought about where they were going and who they were meeting. "Not casual enough?"

For a woman who'd spent five months in maternity pants and then three years in yoga pants, she'd lost the thread on *What are pants?* and *Can I wear these out of the house?*

"Just the right amount of casual," Mom said.

Bea, Helen's three-and-half-year-old daughter, sat at the

kitchen island, eating toast dripping with jam. Bea was a *more is more* kind of kid, especially when it came to jam.

"What do you think, Bea?" Daphne asked, wiping the jam off her daughter's face. "Is something exciting going to happen to Mommy today?"

"No." Bea said her favorite word and shook her head seriously.

"I hope you're wrong kid," Mom muttered.

This was sweet and all, but Helen was kind of having a moment and she needed Mom to focus.

"Does it look like I'm trying too hard? I mean…" Helen pulled the hem of her favorite denim jacket that she legit wore to her first Band of Outlaws concert. And she wore her nearly threadbare Johnny Cash T-shirt. The one with him giving the finger.

That was cool, right?

AND she was she was wearing jeans. Her good ones. The pre-baby, pre-pandemic ones. That she could get them on was miracle and a testament to anxiety as an appetite suppressant.

"I don't want to look like I'm trying too hard."

It was the most rock-and-roll look she had. And she thought it was pretty good. But considering her age and single mom status, did that automatically make it lame? Probably.

Was she overthinking everything? Absolutely.

"Honey?" Mom walked back over to Helen, her beautiful long blond hair was turning silver and she didn't look like she was old enough to be a grandmother. Those good Larson genes. Mom cupped Helen's face in her hands. "You could not be more beautiful. You could not be more capable. You won't throw up on his feet. You're going to be fine." She glanced down at her watch. "And you're going to be late."

As if cued, Helen's stepfather, Jonah, honked the horn in the driveway.

"And listen." Mom leaned in conspiratorially. "If the rumors are true…"

"Which rumors?" Micah Sullivan, lead singer of the Band of Outlaws had a lot of rumors attached to him.

"You know the ones." Mom waggled her eyebrows.

"Mom, in what world do you imagine I'm going to be able to verify *those* rumors?"

"I don't know, honey. He's a rock-and-roll god. Who knows what is going to happen?"

And that, really, was the crux of her stress. She didn't know what was going to happen. And she'd spent the last three-and-half years trying—and in a lot of cases succeeding—in knowing what was going to happen. In some circles she might be called a control freak.

So much so, she hadn't been off this mountaintop in the Catskills for quite a long time.

After Evan died, she'd moved back to her parents' farm with Bea.

She worked doing the fundraising for Haven House, the charity Jonah started on the property adjacent to the farm. Helen literally walked to work. And her social life was over at the Riverview Inn, the inn her uncles, Gabe and Max, had built and still managed, which was twenty minutes away.

She wasn't, like…a shut-in. That would be ridiculous. But between having Bea and then the pandemic, she, well, she didn't go much farther than from the farm to Haven House. And Haven House to the Riverview Inn.

Which, frankly, was more ground, and more room, than lots of people'd had in the pandemic.

But still.

"Helen," Mom said. "Jonah is waiting, and the man is going to lose his cool."

"Right." Because if Helen loved Band of Outlaws, Jonah was borderline obsessed. And this was a fantastic opportunity—not just for her and for Haven House fundraising, it was a big deal to her beloved stepfather.

Life is hard; you don't have to make it harder—that was something her cousin Josie had said to her when she'd been freaking out about moving back in with her parents. And it had become her mantra, of sorts.

Who cared if she was cool? Who cared if she threw up on Micah Sullivan's shoes? This was about Haven House and Jonah. Not her.

"Okay, we'll be back later, Mom."

"Have fun," Daphne said, and Helen turned and hit the screen door. She practically ran down the steps across the dirt driveway to Jonah's truck. She jumped into the passenger seat and clipped on her seat belt.

"Helen?" Jonah said. And she looked over at her stepdad with his more salt than pepper hair and his eyes that always saw everything. "You ready?"

"So ready."

Jonah hit Play on his phone and peeled out of the driveway, dirt obscuring the view of the farm and Haven House behind them.

They took the back roads as far as they could and Helen didn't say a word when he got up on the highway. She slipped her sunglasses down over her eyes and wrapped her fingers around the seat belt.

And she was fine. Totally fine.

She turned up the volume on the radio and Micah Sullivan's voice—that magical combination of gravelly and smooth—filled the cab of the truck.

"Is that too loud?" she yelled at Jonah.

"Just right," he yelled back.

Band of Outlaws lived in that sweet spot between rock and country, but Micah's voice conveyed so much emotion that he got asked to be on all kinds of duets. He did one with Ariana Grande that had just won a Grammy. And during the worst of the pandemic he'd done all kinds of unexpected duets on social media. Country stars, rap stars, hip hop, k-pop, even one with Bangledeshi pop star Runa Laila. And he would do guitar lessons every morning, teaching Band of Outlaws songs in his sun-splashed bedroom with his hair a mess, a cup of coffee steaming on the table beside him.

Rumpled and notoriously unsmiling with the unmade bed behind him, it was a whole mood. And Helen didn't play guitar but she tuned into that live stream every morning.

It was...*he* was...a real lifeline during those dark days.

A hot, sexy, rock-and-roll dream-come-true lifeline.

He'd written the new album during the pandemic and now the band was about to go on tour.

The song switched and Jonah turned it down. "I still can't believe this is happening."

"You and me both, Jonah."

"Did he say how he heard of Haven House?"

She shook her head. A month ago she'd gotten an email from what seemed like Micah Sullivan's personal email, saying he would like to donate money to Haven House and asking if he had the right person.

At first she'd thought it was a scam, but after a moment's quiet freak-out, she'd replied, that yes, she was the right person, but was this *THE* Micah Sullivan? He'd replied with the amount he'd like to donate—which gave her another freak-out—that he would like it to be anonymous and that his manager would be in touch with information so she could come and watch the band rehearse in White Plains for their upcoming tour.

Just so you know I'm real. That's what he'd said. *Just so you know I'm real.*

And then a personal check had arrived for one hundred thou-sand dollars, signed by Micah.

"Your mother thinks it's community service for that bar fight he got into in Albany last year. Or the one this year."

Micah Sullivan got into a lot of fights. Dive bars in small

towns. In airports. Once legendarily while on stage at his own concert.

Helen and Jonah had a whole narrative about this in their heads, about how he went to dive bars to try and get away from his fame and whatever, but someone there always recognized him and started shit. Micah tried to walk away but some yokel wouldn't have it.

There was no way Micah was the kind of guy who started fights. He was the kind of guy who ended up having to defend himself.

Though that didn't explain the airports.

Or backstage at the Grammys.

Whatever. It was a character flaw in her imaginary boyfriend she was able to look past.

"He can't just want to give to a good cause?" she asked. Haven House was an excellent cause.

"Of course. I just don't know how he heard of our good cause," Jonah said.

Years ago, when Jonah came into Helen and Daphne's lives, he brought with him Haven House. A place for single mothers to go with their kids, to get job training, counseling, and education, and most importantly, a chance to rest and recover with their children in a beautiful mountain resort. Over the years it had grown and flourished, and when Helen started to work for Haven House as director of communications and fundraising, she'd increased their reach by about a million.

"He heard of us because I've been working my ass off for two years."

"You have," Jonah said, letting go of the wheel with one hand to clap it on hers. "You totally have. I do not mean to imply you haven't."

She smiled and tried not to freak out and tell him to keep both hands on the wheel. She glanced sideways out the window as the countryside morphed into suburbia. Every once in a while there would be one hold-out farm. A red building with a few horses outside surrounded by a moat of green grass and fields, with gas stations and office buildings right at the edge.

The people on those farms, were they foolish? Or brave? Holding on to something everyone around them had let go of.

She shook her head and looked back over at Jonah.

"I think it was his manager who found us," she said. "She's probably got a finger on New York State charities." For court-mandated community service purposes.

"Yeah," Jonah said. "You're probably right."

"But if it makes you feel better, let's say he read that piece in *Eastern New York* magazine or *Women's Day*—"

"Or the *New York Times*," Jonah protested. She stiffened. That *New York Times* piece last year hadn't been so much about Haven House as it was about her and the court case and her very public moment. Every time she thought about it she wanted to puke and cry.

"Sure. He read it, was impressed by what we're doing and reached out a year later."

Jonah smiled and nodded. "Yeah. Let's go with that. What's your plan?"

"What do you mean?" she asked

Jonah shot her a look. "I mean, you're going to take his donation and then what…?"

"Thank him."

"Helen. Please. I know you. I've watched you work. When you and Evan—"

"That was political fundraising," she said. She no longer flinched when she heard Evan's name. She wondered when that happened. It seemed like she'd let go of something without even realizing it.

"I know you've got more planned," Jonah said, and Helen kept her mouth shut for, oh…eight seconds.

"I'm going to ask him to come and perform at the Haven House picnic."

"Oh my god, seriously?" Jonah asked, and his look of horror and excitement mirrored exactly how she felt.

"Yep. I'm going to ask the biggest music star in the world to come and sing at the picnic in September. And maybe—"

"No. Don't."

"Sign some autographs."

"Helen." He sounded like Helen's teenage sister Iris. It was adorkable.

"And be a part of the auction."

"Like donate a guitar or something?"

"Sure. If that's what he wants."

"That auction…" Jonah shook his head. The auction, another thing that had grown since she'd been running it—two years on line and last year in person. People donated all sorts of things, but what it had suddenly become famous for, thanks to the Athens Fire Department, was…bachelors. Bachelor fire fighters donating their time. Not in a gross way, she made sure of that. There were no candlelit dinners or stripper music. There were handyman services and lawn care. Eaves trough clearing and property clean-up. Last year two guys donated the design and building of a tree house.

It was all very wholesome, but the auction had gotten some press, and because it was for a charity for single moms, some of that press took the cheeky route and…well, The Haven House Bachelor Auction was now a *thing*. And she would have stopped it, if that had been necessary to preserve the integrity of Haven House. But she was glad it hadn't been necessary, because it raised a lot of money. And it was fun.

And, as she was trying to remind herself on a daily basis—not everything needed to be serious all the time.

"An hour music lesson with Micah Sullivan?" she said. "An hour private concert?"

"I'd bid on those."

"Everyone will bid on those."

The song switched and Band of Outlaws' biggest hit, the song

Micah had sung with Juliette St. James four years ago, filled the truck. Helen had to imagine that there were ten thousand couples who'd planned to use that song for their weddings–she and Evan had been one of them.

The second he realized what it was, Jonah fumbled for the phone.

"It's all right," she said, when he accidentally turned the music off instead of just fast-forwarding the song.

"I'm sorry. I forgot I put it on there."

"It's a good song," Helen said. "Go ahead and play it."

"Helen."

"You think they won't be playing it today?" she asked.

"I could ask him not to." He was joking, but not really. Jonah would ask one of the biggest music stars in the world not to play his biggest hit because it reminded her of Evan and made her cry.

Her diaphragm unseized and she laughed. She laughed harder than his little joke warranted, but she was just barely hanging on. She was white-knuckling this whole thing. A semi truck passed on the left and their truck did that little shimmy in its wake. She gripped the seat belt so hard the edges cut into her skin.

"Helen," Jonah said in that quiet voice she'd heard so often in the last couple of years and she shook her head.

"Don't want to cry, Jonah. Just play the next song."

Band of Outlaws' guitars and drums filled the car and then so did Micah Sullivan's voice, not a great voice, probably, but somehow *perfect* all the same.

Perfect for songs about loss and love and waking up every morning hoping shit would get better.

It was no wonder she loved the music so much; it spoke right to her soul.

As Jonah drove five miles per hour below the speed limit behind an SUV, hurtling toward a rehearsal space in White Plains, she closed her eyes and clung to Micah's voice and his lyrics the way she had for the last few years.

CHAPTER
Two

MICAH

Danny was off. He wasn't just off… he was…playing an entirely different song? Micah could feel his brother Alex staring death arrows at him. Micah turned slightly and looked over at Danny, sitting on top of the speaker, looking down at his bass, like they were in conversation.

Which was lovely. And classic Danny.

It was just the wrong fucking conversation.

"Stop!" Micah yelled into the mic. "Stop. Danny? You all right, mate?"

Danny Singh looked up through his long dark hair and blinked. His smile was the exact smile of a kid getting a bike for Christmas. He was barely twenty-one. It was absolutely criminal that the guy was so young and so talented. Micah knew bringing Danny in on bass was a risk, but he'd expected the kid's talent and personality to win over the rest of the band.

He was wrong.

"If we slowed it down…" Danny said.

"Oi!" Sean MacNee on the drums shouted. "We're not slowing down any more songs, Danny! We're a rock band, not a..."

"But listen, if we slowed it down it's a riff on Handel's *Messiah*—"

"What the hell, Micah?" Alex, Micah's half-brother and whole pain in the ass, and the lead guitar player for the band, came up on his left. He didn't even bother to lower his voice and Danny could hear him. "I know you like the guy, but this—"

"Shut up, Alex."

"Micah?"

"I'm serious." He turned to face his brother and saw what he always did. They shared the same eyes. Mom's eyes. They shared Mom's musical ability, too. And her quick temper.

But Alex had his father's black hair and shit-eating grin.

And cruel streak.

Alex was seven years younger than Micah. Eons younger. Worlds younger. They'd had very different versions of the same mother growing up, and that had made all the difference.

"We've been over this," Micah whispered to his brother, his hand over the microphone. "Danny stays."

"He was amazing in the studio with the new album. And in that online shit you were doing. I can't argue that. But live?"

"He'll be fine. We just need to practice and that's what we're doing."

"What is going on with you, Micah?" Alex asked.

"What are you talking about?"

"You've been a fucking pill since the lockdown. You're pissed all the time."

"I'm not pissed."

"At me, you are." Alex's eyebrows lifted, daring him to say different. Micah couldn't argue. "Right. And now, bringing in some unknown bass player? The tone of this whole album—"

"There's nothing wrong with the album."

Alex sighed. "We're Band of Outlaws, Micah. We're not *your* band and you're treating us like we are."

"Micah?" Jo, the band manager, approached the stage from the door. The rehearsal space was huge and it took her minutes to get to a spot where she could talk to him without yelling.

"What's up, Jo?" he asked, once she was close enough. Jo was terrifying. Half drill sergeant, half high school principal, she took no shit and kept them all in line. And they, like the children they were, loved and resented her for it.

"The Haven House people?"

He blinked and felt that spike of adrenaline.

"They're here?"

"Just parked outside. An older man and a young woman. I have their names…" She paged through her phone.

Jonah and Helen. He knew their names.

"Okay, great. Thanks." Micah turned back to the band who were watching him with furrowed brows. "It's a charity thing," he said by way of explanation, and really that was all he was going to say.

"Let's take 'Now or Never' from the top. Danny?"

"I'm good," their new bassist said with an awkward smile.

"Just play the fucking song, yeah?" Sean said.

"You bet!" Danny gave an awkward thumbs-up that Micah found completely endearing. Sean rolled his eyes and Alex, to his left, swore under his breath. Danny did not fit anyone's idea of a rock and roll hero, but the guy was a virtuoso. Like, a legit musical genius. And since Miguel, their original bassist, still wasn't cleared to go on tour, Danny would be a fine replacement for a few months until Miguel got back on his feet.

Behind him, at the door, he heard the murmur of voices, Jo welcoming people into the rehearsal space. Micah felt the tingle of dread and excitement. That delicious buzz of what might be amazing or might be disaster. Chaos. The unknown in all its complexity.

Fuck. He loved it.

He kept his back to the door and caught the eyes of his band. Sean lifted his stick, gave it a twirl and counted them in to their newest song. Danny, watching Sean, came in with that bass line that felt like sex and flight all at the same time. Then it was Alex, with those high runs across the top of the scale.

Micah came in, steady and loud. He wasn't a great guitar player, but he was steady and loud.

He kept his back to the door, focused on the band. But he was aware. So fucking *aware*. Of Jonah.

Helen.

The past he'd spent the last fifteen years running from, and now he was inviting it in.

Somehow, in his darkest moments, Helen Larson had reached into his life and pulled him back from an abyss. Twice. And she didn't even know.

This is only going to go bad, he thought with that same reckless joy fighting gave him.

And he started to sing.

Micah felt that curtain get drawn around the band. There was something that came from surviving the dizzying climb to stardom and then clinging to it with everything they had. It was trial by fire and they'd nearly lost their grip a dozen times. They'd spent the last six years singing into the screaming faces of fans, leaving their blood, sweat and tears on stages around the world.

And they sounded fucking great.

And Helen was here. Seeing it.

No lie, it was enough to get a guy hard.

"Jesus, Danny!" Alex shouted as the music fell apart like a half-built house coming down around their ears.

"No," Sean said. "That was me."

The spell broken, Jonah turned and found himself staring at the two people next to Jo at the door.

Jonah looked the same, a little older, but still tall and trim and serious-eyed. He'd been a runner, Jonah remembered that about him. And asthmatic, the kind of contradiction Micah could get behind. And next to him...

Helen.

She was blond and small. Freckled. She looked nervous. Unsure. She tucked hair behind her ear in exactly the same way he remembered about her, and it was like being kicked in the balls.

Look at me. Remember me.

She turned away.

And *that* was like being kicked in the balls.

"From the top," Micah shouted and they went into it again. Drums, bassline, guitar. Voice.

What did he think was going to happen? Really? She'd take one look at him and remember everything?

Helen

"This is first song on the new album," said the very nice but extremely businesslike woman with the phone and the clipboard, shouting over the guitars and the drums being played on the stage a hundred feet away.

"It's awesome," Jonah said.

Helen nodded but…well, it wasn't awesome. It was loud. And it felt sharp. She could feel Jonah looking at her, waiting for her to say something about Haven House. And Micah's donation. But the music was making a mess of her head. She felt like the five top layers of her skin were gone and her nerves were exposed. She couldn't actually *look* at the band.

"I'm Jonah," Jonah said, stepping into the conversational gap. "One of the executive directors of Haven House."

"Nice to meet you. I'm Jo Hayes, manager of the band."

"That must be quite a job," Jonah said with a laugh. He glanced Helen's way, waiting for her to kick into gear. "This is my daughter, Helen. She's in charge of well, basically everything."

"Sure. I understand that job," Jo said, with a tight smile. "Nice to finally meet you."

She and Jo had been emailing back and forth over this visit.

Helen wasn't sure what her face was doing. Was she smiling? She nodded but then couldn't seem to stop.

"Band of Outlaws start a North American tour in three months," Jo said over the guitars. "They kick off the tour in Madison Square Garden."

"I got the update," Jonah said. "So excited. I'm a huge fan. And I'll be taking my wife to the show."

"We'd be happy to provide you some tickets."

"Oh!" Jonah looked so thrilled. So shocked. It was sweet. *Oh my god, am I still nodding?* Helen wondered. "That would be so kind. We appreciate it! "

Jo smiled. "We'd love to give you two tickets, too," Jo said to Helen, and the tears came out of the blue. Hot and mean at the back of her eyes, and bile was suddenly thick in her throat.

I don't need two tickets.

"Helen?" Jonah whispered and she saw this scene from outside her body. Jo, oblivious, was looking at her phone, but then catching some strange vibe in the air, looked over at Helen. Her eyes grew wide with awareness that something was wrong. That Helen was, in fact, about to cry or vomit or both.

"It's all right," Jo said, putting a hand on Helen's arm that felt terrible. "Lots of people get starstruck."

Oh, God. That was worse. Infinitely worse.

"Can you point me in the direction of the bathroom?" Helen asked with a smile that felt more like a grimace.

"Third door on the left," Jo said, pointing right outside the doorway. "Just past the closet." The rehearsal space was sort of round so the hallway curved out of sight.

Helen left, the music becoming indistinct as she put some distance between herself and the instruments. She just needed a breath. Some cold water on her face. Some dark and some quiet.

She was fine. Totally fine.

Behind her, the music stopped and she heard Jonah's laugh. Awkward and too loud.

He's meeting Micah, that's why he's laughing like that. It made her feel incredibly tender toward her stepdad, but nauseous all the same.

Third door. She pulled it open and found a big dark closet. It held a bucket and four hanging coats.

"Helen?" Jonah shouted.

And it wasn't the smartest thing she'd ever done. It made very little sense. But she went into the closet and closed the door behind her, the dark slipping over her like cool, refreshing water.

I'll be fine. I just need a second.

She closed her eyes and repeated that like a mantra.

Minutes later the door to the closet opened, cutting a slice out of the darkness and she undoubtedly looked like a mole person blinking into the light and the familiar face of Micah Sullivan.

Well. Shit.

MICAH SULLIVAN WAS *BEAUTIFUL*. Like, for real, beautiful. But a different kind than the pictures of him in magazines.

This real-life version of him was infinitely more interesting. His sandy blond hair hung down in messy waves to his shoulders and those famous blue eyes were darker than she'd thought. Dark blue. Like old denim. But he had wrinkles around them, like he'd spent some time squinting into the sun. There was that infamous scar that ran down through his right eyebrow, that came from a beer bottle smashed against his head when he was twenty-one.

His nose had been broken a time or two. And his jaw was covered in a patchy beard that gave him the look of a Civil War soldier.

The effect, all in all, was very serious. Nearly stern. A man who'd seen some shit.

But his lips. His beautiful, thick, puffy lips. The lips were a law unto themselves. Too much, really. But they gave his rather beaten-up face a softness.

An almost outrageous sexiness.

"Hi," she said, stupidly, because she was in a closet. Thinking about Micah's lips.

"You okay?"

"Totally," she lied. "You?"

He smiled.

Helen had seen some things. Some beautiful things. But, good lord forgive her, her child's first smile was NOTHING on Micah Sullivan's grin. It was so beautiful it robbed her of brain cells.

"I thought the closet was a bathroom," she said.

"You're not using it as a bathroom, are you?"

"No!" she said. "Just…taking a second."

She pulled the edges of her denim jacket down and took a breath. She wasn't ready to get out of the closet, but clearly the time had come.

"I'm Helen," she said.

"Micah."

She laughed. "I know."

"Micah?" Jo's voice came around the bend of the hallway.

"I think that's our cue," Helen said and stepped around the bucket to get out of the closet, but to her surprise, Micah stepped in and shut the door behind him.

"You're not…*you're* not using it as a bathroom, are you?" she asked. And then wanted to die. *You just asked Micah Sullivan if he was going to pee in a closet.*

"No. Those days are behind me," he said. "I gave up tequila and I stopped peeing in closets."

Laughter kind of burbled out of her. There was a bright line of light coming in from under the door, covering them in shades of shadow.

"You do this a lot? Hide in closets?" he asked, his voice dropped to a whisper.

"No. Not really. It's new," she whispered back.

"Just something you're trying out?"

"Yeah. What about you?"

"What about me?"

"Aren't you hiding in here, too?"

"I guess so."

Someone walked past the closet, making the light under the door go dark for a second.

"Micah!" Jo yelled again in the hallway.

"Are you—"

"Shhhh," he said.

"Are you scared of your manager?" she whispered.

"Very."

She laughed, as silently as she could, and in the light coming up from under the door she saw his smile.

The corkscrew of anxiety slowly unwound, sped up, maybe, by the sheer shock of her current circumstance.

I'm in a closet with Micah Sullivan.

She glanced down and realized her fingers were just a few inches away from the fingers that had written "This Is Forgiveness," and "What Happens Next" and "When I See You."

"I had a panic attack," she said, and then wished she hadn't. "I mean…that's why I'm here. I had a panic attack and went looking for the bathroom and found the closet."

"Close enough?"

"Something like that."

In the dark he was silent and the quality of his silence was… well, it was excellent. Some people's quiet felt like pressure. Or worse, judgment. His was…neither.

"Do you have them a lot?"

"Panic attacks?"

She felt more than saw him nod.

"More than I'd like," she said, as if it was a joke.

"Are you feeling better?" he asked.

"I am. Thank you."

"I hope it wasn't caused by me?" he asked. "The panic attack?"

"Do a lot of people get panic attacks when they meet you?"

"You wouldn't believe what some people do when they meet me," he said. And she realized his smile wasn't so much an actual smile but the appearance of a smile. Like he was able to convey a full smile with the quirk of his mouth. That was an interesting trick. "But most people aren't actually meeting me, you know. The ones that cry or throw up or, I don't know…hide in closets. They are meeting their memories or whatever my music reminds them of. Their first cars and first crushes. They're meeting the fight they had with their dad or the way their cigarettes used to smell or sex used to feel."

She made a noise when he said the word *sex* and it was honestly only because she was human, and the sexiest man living had said the word sex right in front of her and she…well, she made a noise. A kind of squeak.

Is it hot in here? It's totally hot in here.

"So?" he asked. "What are you actually meeting when you meet me?"

She wouldn't say it. She didn't owe him that. She didn't owe anyone Evan's name, or his memory. The silence in the closet stretched taut. The heat going cold.

She could feel him looking at her and she didn't understand why he was interested. It didn't make any sense. He was Micah Sullivan, about to go on a worldwide tour with his uber-famous band, and she was Helen Larson, who'd just been on the highway for the first time in years.

"You should get back," Helen said. "Your band is probably looking for you."

He reached up and pulled the light string. The bulb was dim and gave the man a kind of glow—one that he probably had anyway. She hoped in the back of her mind that she had the same kind of glow, too.

"They absolutely are," he said with the grin she'd seen flashed across dozens of magazines. "But you can stand in this closet for as long as you need to."

What did it say about her life that that was the sweetest thing that had been said to her in years? The strange kindness of Micah Sullivan would be something she would never forget.

"I'm okay. Thank you." She reached for the door to let them out.

"Helen. I need to tell you—" He put a hand on her arm, and through the denim and her grief and years of loneliness she felt the weight of his hand, the pressure of his touch, and made another gaspy squeak.

"Sorry," he said, and pulled his hand back.

She threw open the closet door, blinked into the sunshine. Gasped for fresh air. The hallway was empty, *thank god*. Because she would not live this down if Jonah knew she'd just spent five minutes in a closet with Micah Sullivan.

She turned and smiled at Micah, though she could not meet his eyes. "I wanted to sincerely thank you for the fantastic donation to Haven House. We are putting the money towards our summer picnic—"

"The summer picnic," he said, stepping into the hallway and shutting the door behind him, and it was like the closet had never happened.

"It's a celebration and a fundraiser event all in one. We have a silent auction and then a larger…auction. And your money will go towards entertainment for kids."

"Bouncy castles?"

"Yes. Exactly." She gave him a wide smile and then got lost for a second in the grin he gave her back. "And because of you we can have a small stage with a magician and musicians." Even though she was really trying not to, her eyes met his. Goodness, they were very pretty eyes. So blue. And those thick, stubby lashes that looked like he was wearing eyeliner. Wait…was he wearing eyeliner?

"Kids love bouncy castles and magicians."

"Indeed, and," she said, warming up to her pitch, "parents love—"

"Micah!" From down the hallway there was a bellowing voice that belonged to a man who was clearly out of patience. "The fuck?"

There was the stomp of boots in the hallway and around the corner appeared Alex Sullivan, Micah's younger brother. If Micah was handsome in a rough-hewn kind of way, Alex was…pretty.

Same blue eyes set in a face that had not been in as many fights. He had jet-black hair, slightly curly and entirely messy. And his smile was well-practiced mischief backed by kilotons of star power.

Helen had to work to keep her jaw from dropping to her chest and her panties from slipping right off her body.

"Oh," Alex said when he saw her. "Sorry. I didn't mean to interrupt anything."

The way he said it. Cheeky and slightly—just a little—sneering, made her spine stiffen.

"You didn't," Micah said, stern again. All softness gone. "Don't be an ass."

Alex held his hands up. "Sorry. Didn't mean to offend anyone. I'm Alex."

"Helen," she said and waved instead of shaking his hand. Which could be seen as a little relic from COVID.

"She's from Haven House," Micah said.

"Well, nice to meet you," Alex said. "But we need our lead singer back."

"Of course." She held up her hands. "Thanks for your time, Micah."

The two men turned from her, and she was a grown woman and a professional, but it would take a woman a million times stronger not to check out their asses as they walked away.

Micah's wins, she thought.

As if she'd said it out loud, Micah turned around and winked at her.

Four

"THAT WAS AMAZING," Jonah said for perhaps the millionth time since leaving the rehearsal space. "The new songs sounded good, didn't they?"

Helen stopped furiously tapping out an email on her phone and looked over at him. "I think they sounded good, but different."

"Good different."

"Intense different."

The good-old-boy lean to some of their music was gone and the new album sounded like a man coming to grips with really hard things. Life-or-death things. Every song was a *moment*. Which was amazing. And also intense.

"I loved that forgiveness song," Jonah said, and she nodded, picking her phone back up. "Did it sound familiar to you?"

"No," she said.

"What about "White-Knuckled"? None of that…"

"What?"

"Sounded familiar?"

"Why in the world would it sound familiar?"

He shrugged.

The truth was that she'd listened to the new songs for a

minute and then retreated into her brain, where the lyrics couldn't touch her and her complicated relationship with forgiveness was left unprodded. Unexamined.

Which was just the way she liked it.

Bursting into tears *on top* of hiding in a closet? Man, there was only so much social disaster in front of an international rock star a girl could handle in one day.

She was aware that it was beginning to rain; the world outside the car windows was going gray and wavy. And the panic she'd expected to feel didn't arrive. It was as if all her adrenaline had gone for the moment. She'd used it up in that closet.

Which wasn't the way it worked, but whatever.

"What are you doing?" Jonah asked.

"I am writing an email to Micah," she said, tapping away. Her thumbs were highly tuned instruments at this point. "I didn't get a chance to pitch my ideas to him, but I think he'd be agreeable to donating some things to the auction."

Thank you, she wrote. *You were kinder than you needed to be today. And I appreciate that more than I can say. You are not at all what I thought. I hope my asking for more of your time and talent doesn't offend you. It's just my job Feel free to email me back at this address or you can reach out on my cell phone.*

She added her cell phone number at the bottom of the email and hit Send.

"There," she said. "Done."

"What a day." Jonah sighed.

"Yep," she said. "It was quite a day."

Her phone binged in her lap and she picked it up to see a message from an unknown number.

What did you expect? When you met me?

"Oh my god," she said, staring down at the text that could only be from one person. A lightning bolt went through her and her fingers tingled. Her whole body tingled with the reappearance of adrenaline and shock.

"What? What's wrong?" Jonah asked.

"Nothing. Micah is just…well, we text now."

"He's texting you?" Jonah asked, his eyebrows lost in his hair. "Like…right now?"

"Yeah." She laughed, feeling giddy and…alive. There was a different chemistry to this. Something that felt like flirtation. Which was ridiculous, she understood that. Micah Sullivan, Rockstar, would not…flirt with her. But also, it seemed like he was? "Hold on."

More growling she texted back, trying to make a joke. But then she settled on the truth. Because it had been that kind of day. *But mostly I didn't expect you to get in that closet with me. Thank you for that.*

The little dots showed up and then disappeared. Showed up. And then disappeared. And then stayed disappeared.

"Well," she said with a sigh, disappointed, though she knew she shouldn't be. "That didn't last long."

They drove past the driveway to the farm.

"Jonah? Where are we going?"

"To the inn."

"They going to make a big deal about this?"

"What?" Jonah looked over at her, like he didn't understand what she was saying. "Make a big deal? Alice? Delia? Your mom? When do they make a big deal about anything?"

The answer was *always*.

The problem with living with her family in such close proximity was that everything was celebrated. Birthdays, anniversaries, promotions, good grades. All of it was celebrated. And to think that this, her and Jonah going to go meet their favorite band, and the first time she'd successfully been in a car on the highway, had left the twenty-mile radius of the farm and the inn, wouldn't be celebrated?

Yeah, she wasn't that naive.

Someone was baking a cake and making a special dinner, and all of her family would have a barrage of questions about meeting Micah and the rest of the Outlaws.

The closet she would keep a secret. Even though Mom and Aunt Alice would lose their minds. It would almost be worth it to see the expressions on their faces, but the follow-up questions would be relentless.

The rain was gone and the anxiety she felt that made the world feel scary sometimes was, for whatever reason, not present.

"What are you thinking?" Jonah asked.

"I'm thinking…" She sighed and didn't give herself to second-guess this instinct. She'd been talking herself out of ideas in the name of safety and being a new mom and the world being a relatively terrifying place for too long. It wasn't her natural state. "That I would like to drive."

He blinked and immediately pulled over to the side of the road. It was twenty minutes from where they were to the inn, along an almost entirely empty road. The rain had left puddles that they avoided as they got out, passing each other at the front of the car.

Jonah, like she was sixteen all over again and he was teaching her how to drive, held out his hand as he jogged past her and she gave him a high five. Laughing like the kid she'd been a lifetime ago.

Settling into the driver seat she felt giddy. Jonah, always intuitive, said nothing as she put the car in Drive and eased off the gravel shoulder onto the old asphalt she practically knew by heart.

In her life before, she used to do a lot of the driving while Evan sat in the passenger seat and sent emails and texts, or sometimes took notes while the two of them hammered out ideas and plans and initiatives.

In her life before, she'd liked driving, particularly on these old mountain roads with their lazy curves and small dips and rises. When she and her cousin Josie were teenagers, they used to drive one of Josie's stepdad's old farm trucks to the top of the highest hill on the north end of the road and gun it down the hill, then whoever was driving would take her foot off the gas and see how far they could coast.

Teenagers thinking they were invincible, obviously. Finding out differently had been a painful lesson.

She drove carefully, her heartbeat normal. Her hands a little sweaty. But okay.

I'm okay.

"Put on some music, would you?" she said.

Jonah immediately played "Wild Horses" by Band Of Outlaws, and Micah's voice, so familiar to her before today, was somehow even more intimate. Like he was singing to her inside that closet.

What a day, she thought. *What a weird and fabulous day.*

CHAPTER

Five

MICAH

When he'd been 12, his mother picked him up from school in the beat-up blue Datsun that was more rust than paint. And she'd been crying, but that wasn't really anything new. And he'd gotten in trouble at lunch, and that wasn't really anything new.

But she'd looked at him with her pretending face. And her pretending face scared him.

"We're going on vacation," she told him, wiping her eyes and her nose.

"Where's Alex?"

"He's staying with Peter. This is just for us."

There'd been a lot of *just for us* things lately. It was making him nervous. Peter wasn't a bad guy but there had been talk about Mom and Peter getting married and Peter adopting him. They fought about it at night and Micah'd heard Peter say "Not unless you get your shit together." A lot.

They drove four hours into the country, away from everything he knew, and that wasn't totally a bad thing.

Finally, they pulled into gravel driveway and a nice man with glasses came out to greet them. But he took one look at Mom and went back into the house. A woman in scrubs came out with him. They helped Mom out of the car and the guy with glasses came around to Micah's side of the car and smiled and said everything was fine.

But he had a pretending face, too.

Micah watched the woman in the scrubs lead his mom into a building. The whole back of Mom's shirt was dark with sweat.

"Is she okay?" he asked the guy in glasses.

"She's going to be fine."

Yeah, he'd heard that before.

"What's your name, son?" the man asked.

"Michael." No one really called him that, but he didn't want this guy to know him. Whatever this was, he didn't want it to be real.

He got out of the car and ran past the man with glasses to the building Mom had gone into. The man with glasses stopped him from going inside. And he wanted to punch this guy with the glasses, but his mom was in that building and he couldn't be sent away.

And that's what happened when you punched an adult.

He learned that at his last school.

The guy with glasses offered to make him a sandwich and an ice cream sundae. A dog came by with a wet nose and wagging tail but he didn't care.

"You can sit out here," the man with glasses finally said, and pointed to some chairs. "Until the nurses are done taking care of your mom, and then you can go see her."

He turned to the guy with glasses. "Can I be alone, please?"

The man blinked behind his glasses and then he finally did what Micah asked. And Micah sat alone on that chair waiting for his mom until he started to think… maybe he should just leave. Just run out into that forest behind them. One of the things mom and Peter always fought about was the trouble he got into in school. His behavior was part of the shit Peter wanted Mom to get together. Maybe, he thought, it would be easier for Mom if he wasn't there. He had twenty bucks in his pocket and, he looked around, his guess was there was some shit in these buildings he could steal. He stood up, thinking he'd start in that big yellow farmhouse he could see through the trees.

"Hi," a girl said, coming up the stairs to the porch where he was standing.

"What do you want?" he asked, his heart pounding so hard he felt a little sick.

"Nothing," she said. She was a little older than he was, he guessed. She had blond hair up in a ponytail and red shorts and green eyes. She had boobs; he noticed that. Even in despair, he was aware of her.

"Want one?" she asked and held out a Popsicle.

Grape, his favorite. And he was suddenly starving and thirsty. He took it without thinking. "I'm Helen," she said. "We don't have to talk, but I thought I'd sit out here with you. So you're not alone. Is that okay?"

Maybe it was the Popsicle, or the way the sun made her eyes glow, or the fact that he didn't want to run away. Not really. He sat. He ate the Popsicle.

She stayed with him for hours.

It had been one of the nicest things anyone had ever done for him. Still was, in a lot of ways. It was the first time she'd saved him.

And she didn't remember.

Thank you for getting in that closet with me.

It was fine that she didn't remember. Expected, even. There'd been a lot of road between that week when he was a kid and right now. If he told her his real name…she might pull up the memory, but he doubted it. She had other things on her mind.

He sat on the edge of the stage with his thumbs over the screen, ready to say something. But in a rare moment for Micah Sullivan, he didn't know what to say.

You're beautiful. And brave. I'm sorry for everything that happened to you.

I want to meet you in a closet again.

"Hey!" Alex came into the rehearsal space and Micah put his phone in his pocket, and he didn't do it in any kind of cool way, but instead in a kind of *I'm trying to hide something from you* way, and Alex, the asshole, saw it.

Alex, when he was being an asshole, saw everything.

Is every little brother like this? Micah wondered. *Or was it their own special magic?*

"What's up?" he asked Alex.

"Jo's calling the cars."

Rehearsal was over. Danny's first day had not gone great.

"You going back into the city?" Alex asked. Micah nodded. He'd been calling New York City home for a few years. They'd been touring so hard for the year before the pandemic that he had no fixed address. When it all shut down he'd been in NYC, so it turned into home.

Alex split his time between his dad's place in Virginia and Micah's place. Reluctant, even in a global pandemic, to put down roots.

"You want to come back with me?" Micah asked, because he knew his brother was waiting for the invite.

"If it's cool?"

Little brothers, right?

"Sure."

"Hey." Alex grinned. "What's the deal with the girl?"

"What girl?" Micah asked, standing to pack up his guitars. They had crew for this, but he needed something to do.

"Don't fuck with me. The charity case."

Micah bristled but didn't give his brother the reaction he was after. "She represents a charity. I'm donating money to the charity. That's all."

"Didn't look like that was all when I saw you in the hallway."

"Don't be a dick."

"I'm not." Alex laughed. "You want to date a civilian, go right ahead. But you know how that works out."

It didn't, was his point. And he wasn't wrong. Band of Outlaws was about to start a world tour and he had no business thinking anything about Helen Larson. It was just that he couldn't stop thinking about Helen Larson.

"Is she the girl? From the article?" Alex asked.

Micah stared at him, stunned he'd connected the dots.

"I've got Google on my phone, man," Alex said. "I looked up Haven House and it was like the fourth thing that popped up."

Micah didn't answer, not wanting to confirm it. Or deny it. Not wanting, really, to look too hard at it.

At the beginning of the pandemic, when the streets were empty and fear was thick in the air, he'd been alone and paralyzed. Absolutely isolated and thinking about drinking. And drinking…drinking was a dead-end for him. Had been since he was fifteen years old. He'd gotten sober after that fight at the Grammy's, and he was doing pretty good. He went to meetings when he needed to. It helped that Miguel, the bass player was sober, too.

But during the lockdown, alone in his apartment, the urge to drink came back so hard. Impossibly hard. It drowned out everything good in his life, especially the music.

He went so far as to have a beer delivered to his apartment. Pabst Blue Ribbon, the kind his mother drank before it was cool. And he'd had maybe a day left of self-control when he read an article in the *New York Times* about Haven House.

About Helen.

What had happened to her. Her fiancé. The trucker who'd fucked up and plowed into his car. The court case and the superhuman thing she'd done.

Part of her victim statement had been in the article, and it was the most beautiful thing he'd ever read.

The cloud had cleared and the music came back to him.

It was the second time Helen had saved him.

It felt like fate. She kept showing up when he needed her most.

He had put the beer out on the stoop to be taken by some lucky teenager and written the new album in a fever dream.

"Does she know?" Alex asked.

Micah shook his head. The album was inspired by her. Some of the lyrics were from her victim statement. He hadn't thought about it at the time, alone in his apartment, when world tours and recording albums felt like they might not happen again.

But now it was all he could think about.

He'd stolen her pain to heal his own.

"Seems like a wasted opportunity if you ask me. You got a real-life muse. Paul McCartney would kick your ass for not immediately marrying her."

Micah laughed without a whole lot of humor.

"You gonna offer her some money?"

He had. He'd given the charity a hundred thousand dollars. And even that didn't make him feel any less guilty. Or any less compelled by her.

"Whatever you do," Alex said. "Don't fuck her."

"Jesus, Alex, I'm not going to fuck her."

"You love complicated shit, man. And this situation has Classic Micah written all over it."

They stood there, him on the stage, Alex on the ground. Micah remembered when Alex was born and Mom had come home from the hospital, looking tired and worn. Peter was a proud father and wanted to be a part of all of it. Diaper changing. Bottles. The sun already beginning to rise and set on Alex's tiny, bald, slightly cone-shaped head. It became obvious real fast how this would all play out.

Alex could do no wrong.

Micah couldn't do anything right.

Whatever Micah had, Alex wanted. And whatever Alex had, Micah disdained. It made for a cage-match childhood.

But Mom had changed everything when she pulled Micah

aside when the writing was on the wall and said *You have to look out for Alex.*

He won't understand responsibility. He just won't.

And Micah had known far too much of responsibility. He'd been a man as a boy. Making sure bills got paid and he was signed up for school.

Micah liked complicated because it was all that was left when he was done looking after his brother.

"She's just a girl," Micah lied. "Let's go home."

CHAPTER

Six

Helen's office was at the very back of Haven House, just off the big industrial kitchen. It made for a lot of noise and interruptions, but she didn't mind. She liked the sound of women's voices laughing and talking, and kids running in and out of her office to the big play room on the other side of the kitchen.

Her daughter, Bea, was sitting in her lap, taking edamame out of the pods and lining them up in front of her on the desk.

"You're supposed to eat those," Helen said into her daughter's curls. She smelled like soap and banana and little-kid sweat from playing hard outside with the other kids before lunch.

"I will," she said, and her chubby fingers split another bean and took out a big fat edamame.

In the last month of her pregnancy, Helen had gone for a while to a widow's support group that met online. She hadn't been married to Evan when he died, but that distinction was meaningless when it came to grief. And she remembered this one woman, Anna, who'd said she couldn't stop attributing everything her children did to her late husband. Every quirk or trait was something her husband had done until she'd written herself right out of the genetic pool.

She'd laughed when she said this, and Helen, so pregnant at the time, couldn't imagine doing that. Going through pregnancy and birth, and then somehow willingly not seeing yourself in your child? Ridiculous.

But she sat here watching her daughter, her nose buried in Bea's chestnut curls (so like Evan's), and watched her daughter methodically pull things apart so she could count and study them, and all she could see was Evan. Evan shining through their daughter.

She understood now, why Anna did it. Because it was comforting to see her beloved and missed Evan alive in some way.

"Hey, Helen?"

Helen spun herself and Bea toward her open office door to find Daniella, the woman who ran the kitchen, standing in her doorway.

"What's up Dani?" Helen asked.

"Mail," she said and handed her a small stack of envelopes.

"Anything good in here?"

"I doubt it. Are we still on for Monday night?"

Bachelor Night.

Every Monday night Dani stuck around to watch *The Bachelor*. They popped popcorn and talked shit to the TV screen and it was the best.

"Actually," Helen said, feeling a giddy stab of bravery. "How about if we watch *The Bachelor* at your house? That way you don't have to stick around here until eight p.m."

"You want to drive to my place?"

It was a thirty-minute drive and Helen didn't have to get on the highway. It was a baby step in the grand scheme of things.

"Yeah, why not?"

Dani blinked at her in a second that stretched. It was a second Helen was familiar with. It was the second after people heard about what happened to Evan. It was the second after people found out she'd had a baby on her own.

This second made her skin itch. It made her want to scream.

She couldn't heal with everyone watching the process.

"That's a great idea," Dani finally said. "If you're cool with it?"

"Totally cool. I wouldn't offer if I wasn't."

"Mom." Bea was now eating all the little edamame beans she had lined up. "Your computer binged."

"I gotta…" Helen held her thumb out toward the computer.

"Go," Dani said. "And yes to Monday at my place."

Helen turned to her computer. There were dozens of emails that she was expecting. Mundane ones. Serious ones. One a shipping confirmation for a new yoga mat she'd ordered. But there was only one she cared about.

It had been a week since she and Jonah went down to watch Band of Outlaws. One week since she'd sent Micah that follow-up email asking for donations for the Haven House Summer Picnic auction.

One week since that one text exchange.

Since the closet.

And she'd heard nothing else. Not one thing.

Not even from Jo about the additional asks.

So, the logical part of her brain was, like…that's that. Nothing more to see there.

But the part of her brain that remembered what he smelled like in that closet was keeping reckless hope alive and every bing that stupid computer made might be him.

Helen kissed her daughter's head and opened up her email.

"Hey," she said. "My yoga mat shipped."

It wasn't until the afternoon that she remembered the mail and ran back to her office to grab it. She had her purse, and Bea was waiting in the kitchen, but she flipped through the mail real quick.

Bills. Garbage. Bills. And then an envelope, soft, the edges crumpled, written on with blue ballpoint pen.

Helen sucked in a breath that got caught in her chest. Lodged somewhere between her lungs and her stomach. The address was her name and Haven House.

Return address was a stamp from Taconic Correctional Facility.

The edges of her vision got blurry and she had to remind herself to exhale.

Breathe. Just breathe.

Twice a year she got these letters from Angela Newman. Maybe there was a chance that they weren't from Angela Newman, but as Angela Newman was the only person she knew from Taconic Correctional Facility, it was a good bet.

The only way to know for sure was to open them. Read them. And she never opened them. Couldn't even dream of reading them.

The hard part of forgiveness was supposed to be the actual forgiving. She'd thought, foolishly maybe, hopefully certainly, that once she'd done it, it would stick. But it seemed to be a process, and there were days it retreated from her like it had never been there. She was left dry and brittle and so full of whatever the opposite of forgiveness was, she was paralyzed.

The letters came to Haven House, and not to the farm, because with her limited resources in jail Angela Newman had googled Helen Larson and found the Haven House address.

If those letters had come to the farm she imagined her parents might throw them away thinking they were protecting her, but because they came here, they didn't even know about them. No one knew about them. And they felt like a dirty rotten secret that someone shoved into her hands. A secret that she'd never wanted, but didn't know how to get rid of. She could tell Dani, of course, to get rid of them. But every time Helen imagined the conversation she couldn't find the words.

So, twice a year, these letters sat, stacked with the bills and junk on Helen's desk. Like a grenade with the pin pulled, just waiting to destroy the little bit of peace and control she'd managed to salvage over the years since Evan died.

And not dealing with the letters wasn't right. She knew that. It was moving her backward and not forward, as her therapist would say if she went to see that therapist anymore. God, she'd never even told the therapist about the letters.

The day the first one came, she'd had a phone call with the *New York Times* to discuss Haven House and its unique fundraising challenges. She'd been so excited about the interview and the chance to talk about the stigma around giving women who lived with poverty—who needed government assistance and often couldn't work because of child-care issues—what some people regarded as a vacation.

But the letter had made a mess of her, and in the interview she'd ended up talking about Angela and what happened to Evan and the victim statement she'd read at the trial. And how forgiveness wasn't stagnant.

And that had become the story.

For weeks she'd felt sick with exposure. Sick with the thought of a million people seeing her pain and pitying her. There'd been calls to go on talk shows and talk to other journalists and she'd ignored them all.

Then it all got drowned out by COVID news.

Weird thing to be grateful for, but here she was, grateful.

And these letters kept coming.

"Mom?" Bea stood in the doorway. She'd insisted on dressing herself this morning and was in head-to-toe orange, including a too-small Halloween shirt.

"Yeah, honey," she said. It took so much work to pretend she was fine. To turn a smiling face on her daughter.

Bea stood there like a pumpkin with curls. "I want to go home."

Helen tore the letter in half before throwing it in the garbage.

"Me too," Helen said, and followed her daughter away from the past.

The Following Monday

The Haven House summer picnic was at the end of September. Back at the very beginning of Haven House, when Jonah, his business partner, Gary, and Mom were really doing just about everything on their own—on top of running a farm and Jonah's real estate empire in the city—they'd wanted to hold it in August but just couldn't get it organized fast enough.

And then they realized the end of September was a much better time to have a picnic in the Catskills. Fewer bugs, better temperatures and all the tourists were gone so the parks belonged to the locals again.

The picnic used to be something that could be put together in a few weeks. Alice and Gabe would donate food and grills. Max and Delia would come down and hang banners, and build the bonfire and the small stage.

But now the event had grown, and thanks to the donation from Micah, Helen was planning the picnic in June. Booking magicians and face painters.

She was expecting close to three hundred people.

"Yes," she said into her phone. She was sitting outside Dani's house Monday night and in a few moments she'd go in to watch *The Bachelor*. She'd driven down by herself. The half hour trip took forty minutes because she got caught behind a tractor and wasn't in the mood to pass it. The trip had, very oddly, not been as hard as she'd thought it would be.

It was actually a little embarrassing how easy it was, and it made her wonder how long she'd been holding on to that fear so needlessly.

Part of it had been the pandemic—she knew that. She'd taken the restrictions seriously—too seriously, the argument could be made.

Healing comes when it comes.

That little nugget of wisdom had been etched on a wine glass.

"Thank you, Chief. That will be great. I'd be happy to have all of you back."

"Please. Helen. I've known you since high school. Call me Shawn."

Fire Chief Shawn Holliwell had been a senior when she was a freshman. And while he wasn't the youngest fire chief the area had ever seen, he was still pretty young. "When I call you Shawn I remember that time you and Cameron climbed up onto the roof of the high school—"

"All right, okay," Shawn said. "We don't need to go that far down memory lane."

Shawn and Cameron had had to be rescued by firefighters, and Shawn always credited that night as having sparked his interest in being one.

"Well, it's something the guys look forward to, and I think we do some good," Shawn said.

She laughed. "Last year the fire department raised five thousand dollars, Chief. So, I'd say, yes. You do some good."

"I'll give the boys the same speech, and we'll put the sign-up sheet in the kitchen. I'll have a list of what the boys are donating to you by the end of the month."

"And we'll start advertising. Thank you, Shawn. And just remind them—"

"I know. I know. Wholesome. Billy really didn't mean anything by the offer of tire rotation. He honestly just meant tire rotation."

She laughed. "I know, Shawn. It's all right."

"Billy was the first one to volunteer again this year," he said, and Helen closed her eyes. "He really enjoys helping you out."

"Chief," she sighed. This again. The whole world had been on a campaign to get her to go out with Billy since the last picnic.

"Ah, we're back to Chief again. I've gone too far. Ignore me, Helen. He's just a nice guy who'd love to take you for a drink."

"And if I was interested in going out for a drink, he'd be a lovely guy to do it with. But I'm not interested in that. With anyone."

"Noted. And I'll get the info to you as soon as I've got it."

They hung up and Helen got out of her car. The front door opened and Dani lifted her arm in a wave.

"Hurry up, the show is about to start," she shouted.

And it was all so normal. So beautifully normal. It was nothing to cry about. But still she blinked away the tears that were part happy and part pride and all embarrassing.

Another Week Later

One of the joys of living on the property of the Athens Organics farm and in the slightly suffocating bosom of her family and extended family and extended, extended family, was that there were endless babysitters. Her younger brothers and sisters, her aunts, Alice and Delia. Her uncles, Max and Gabe. There were so many willing babysitters and so many things to do that between Haven House, the farm and the Riverview Inn, Bea could be found covered in flour baking in the kitchen with Alice, or handing all the wrong tools to Max as he fixed things in the cabins, or examining the first tender green buds of strawberries in the fields.

It was, without a doubt, an absolute blessing.

The other side of living in the bosom of her family was that everyone had an opinion all the time and there was no getting away from it.

"I'm telling you," Alice was telling Daphne as they sat in the huge kitchen of the inn. "It's not as bad as you think." Alice was making a sauce, Helen was peeling potatoes for the night's gnocchi, and Daphne was having a glass of wine and scrolling through a dating site.

"I don't care," Helen said, pointing the peeler at her mother. "I don't care. And if you keep going on like this, you can peel your own damn potatoes."

"This guy looks nice." Daphne tilted the phone toward Helen, who ignored it.

"Let me see," Alice said. Her dark hair had an amazing silver streak through it. She called it her superhero streak. Helen, who wasn't yet thirty, hoped she grew old with the grace of these women around her. Though perhaps without all the know-it-all nosiness. She vowed then and there to just let Bea live her life when it was all said and done. And to never, ever look at dating websites on her behalf.

"Yeah. Hot," Alice said. "And he lives in Catskill."

Graceful and stubborn.

"Stop. I'm *begging* you."

"Fine," Daphne said and put down her phone. "We'll stop."

Helen pushed the peeled potatoes over to her mom to cut and put in the salted, boiling water on the stove.

"You can grow old with me at my house forever and ever," Daphne said.

Helen rolled her eyes.

"And me," Alice said. "You can be our, like, companion. Like we're old Victorian ladies, and you can bring us tea and hold our umbrellas just right so our fair wrinkled skin doesn't get burnt and you can never have sex again."

"Not ever again," Daphne said.

"But we'll have dogs. Lots of dogs," Alice said.

"We don't need any more dogs," Helen said. All of them had dogs now, and it was like wild kingdom when the families all got together. In this strange space between having children out of the house and waiting for grandkids—with all of this love and nurturing to spare—her aunts and uncles had gotten dogs.

Is that going to happen to me? she wondered. *Me and Bea and ten cats?*

Shit. Maybe I should be looking at the dating websites.

"What about that Billy Sorenson from the fire station?" Alice asked. "He so obviously has a thing for you."

"You are the second person to bring up Billy Sorenson! Is he enlisting all of you to get me out on a date?"

"No. I think it's just in the air. You two are young. Attractive. He's a firefighter, for crying out loud. You should be dating."

"He's, like, twenty-five," Helen said.

"And you're eighty?"

"No," she protested and shrugged. "But...you know what I mean."

Billy was a nice guy. And hot. But Billy had grown up around here a cheerful golden boy. He'd played lacrosse in high school and he was voted Homecoming King and everyone had something nice to say about him. There wasn't an edge on him anywhere. There was no darkness. No hint of some heartbreak.

And she couldn't imagine what she would even say to the guy.

"Fair," Alice said and poured more wine into Daphne's glass. "But...you are thinking about it, right?"

"About what?"

"Sex?"

"Oh my god, Aunt Alice!"

"I'm serious. You're too young. Too beautiful. Too smart to be our companion. Some guy out there needs you. And your vagina needs some love."

"My...vagina is fine."

"You can't even say it," Alice said, pointing at her with a wooden spoon. "That's how distanced you are from your vagina, you've forgotten how to say the word. Say it with me, VA—"

"I can't believe this is happening," Helen breathed. "Look. My vagina is fine. No one needs me. And Bea adores me. When did you get so dramatic, Alice?"

"She's always been dramatic," Daphne said. "But she's right. Aren't you lonely?"

"I am surrounded by my family 24/7. Who has time to be lonely?"

"You know what I mean."

"Fine! Yes!" The words popped out of her, unexamined and unrealized. But they were true. "I am lonely."

"Really?" Alice asked, eyes wide.

"This is a weird thing to be happy about," Helen said.

"It's the first step!" Daphne cried and then Alice cheered.

"Stop. Please stop, or you'll bring in—"

As if cued, in walked Uncle Gabe. He was trying out facial hair these days and had a real mountain-man-in-pressed-khakis kind of vibe. It was weird, if you asked Helen, but the way Alice stroked his cheeks would indicate her approval. Alice and Gabe had been married before, but had broken up after years of infertility heartbreak. But when Gabe opened the inn he needed a chef, and Alice had needed a fresh start after her restaurant failed. Neither of them had expected to get back together. And they'd really never expected to have kids. And now Stella was about to graduate high school. And their love had been a huge part of creating the magic of the Riverview Inn.

"What are we cheering about?" Gabe asked, his arm around his wife, his smile for all of them.

"Sports," Alice lied. Gabe laughed.

"Yeah? Which one?"

Alice stroked his beard again. "I don't know. The one with the net?"

"All right," he said. "Keep your secrets. The grill is ready. Are you ready for me to put the pork on?"

"No," Alice said. "We need fifteen more minutes, considering our gnocchi crew is moving slow." Gabe grabbed a wine glass from the tray at the end of the counter and flipped it over for his wife to fill. Alice didn't drink, but it was never a problem when other people did on Sunday night. She'd struggled with alcoholism when she and Gabe split up the first time, and she always said she valued what she had too much to risk it for a drink.

Gabe lifted the bottle toward Helen. "Do you want a glass?"

"Sure," she said.

Maybe I should let Billy take me out for a drink. We don't have to fall in love. Or even have a second drink.

But there had to be a first date after Evan at some point.

With a belly full of delicious gnocchi and salad, she drove Bea home from the inn to the farm. Those twenty minutes on the familiar highway felt good again. Felt like home again. She pulled in under the apple tree and turned the car off.

"Come on, honey," she whispered, lifting her sleeping baby from the car seat and carrying her boneless, sweet-smelling little girl into the farmhouse.

They'd turned the spare bedroom into a room for Bea, complete with a sun painted on the ceiling and a friendly, if lopsided, giraffe on the wall, like she was peeking over the edge of Bea's crib.

Josie had painted it for her.

A sudden pang of missing Josie hit her square in her chest. She wasn't entirely sure where Josie and Cameron were these days. It had been a while since she'd tuned in to their exceedingly popular Five Questions and a Cup of Coffee YouTube channel. It was just called Five Questions when Cameron was doing it by himself, when Josie joined him, she added the coffee part.

The pandemic had been weirdly good to them—everyone home and desperate to watch something to alleviate the boredom of isolation and the high-level anxiety from the news. And there had been Cameron, sitting at a fire, making coffee for extremely famous and interesting people, asking them five sometimes silly, sometimes important, questions.

To say it was going gangbusters was an understatement. During the lockdown he did the interviews over zoom and then socially distanced around fires.

And once they could travel again, they'd loaded up their

camper van and headed south. Or north? They might be in Canada. She honestly couldn't remember.

She stroked Bea's sleep-sweaty head and then pulled her phone from her back pocket and took a picture of Ginny the Giraffe, as Josie had named her, and sent it off to her cousin/best friend.

Ginny says hi. I miss you. Where are you?

She hit Send and put the phone back in her pocket.

She tidied up a few of the toys and books that were scattered across the rug. *Goodnight Goon* and *Chrysanthemum* were current favorites. She was tempted to hide them, just to avoid reading them tomorrow for perhaps the millionth time. But she knew better. Bea would systematically take this room apart to find what she wanted.

Like Evan.

She shook off the memory and took a deep breath in the hushed and darkened room.

Where am I? she thought. *I mean, really. Where am I?*

Her parents' house? Her childhood home? She was about to climb into her childhood bed. And it had been amazing, safe and easy for years. Only just now was it starting to feel like quicksand.

She blew out a breath, shook her head. There was something in the air with her.

"Weird night," she whispered out loud. "It's just a weird night."

The insistent buzz of her phone pulled her out of a deep sleep and a pleasantly surreal dream of watching a monster truck rally with Josie. She opened one eye, saw that it was still dark. Middle-of-the-night dark. She sat bolt upright.

Only bad news came in the middle of the night.

Her brain went crystal clear. Absolutely focused, even as her body broke out in a frigid sweat.

"Hello?" she said into her phone.

"You have a collect call from Monroe County Jail."

Angela Newman

But no. She was in Taconic and Monroe County was Rochester.

Who did she know in Rochester who would be getting arrested?

"Do you accept the charges?"

"Yes."

There was a click and a buzz and then the ambient din of a busy hallway.

"Helen?" a voice said. And it took her a second to place the voice, because there was no scenario in the world she could possibly imagine in which this guy was calling her from jail.

"Micah?!"

Helen

"Yeah."

She blinked. Speechless.

"What…what is happening?"

"Well, I've been arrested. The band is in White Plains and Jo… well, Jo seems to be a bit peeved at the moment."

"So you called me?"

"Yeah."

"Because that made sense to you?"

"I had your number."

"Don't you have like…a million numbers?"

"Actually, no."

There was a click and someone in the background on his end yelled something.

"I'm running out of time, here. Is it possible you could come get me?"

"At the Monroe County Jail?"

"Yes."

"In Rochester."

"I think...I'm not sure about that. Hey man?" he asked someone on his end. "What town are we in...? Yes. Rochester."

"That's, like...hours away from me."

"I understand that. You'll also have to bail me out."

"Bail you out?" She started laughing.

"Helen, we have a time issue at work here, so maybe save your questions for the end?"

"You want to scold the person you're asking to pick you up from jail."

"I'll pay you back, obviously. And donate those items you mentioned in your email to your auction."

She perked right up.

"All of them?"

"I think we can talk about it when you pick me up."

"Am I being blackmailed?"

"Maybe? So far news outlets don't have a hold of this and I'd like to keep it that way, so the sooner the better?"

"None of this explains why I'm the lucky person getting this call." She stood up and started to pull off her pajama shorts.

"I don't have a lot of people to call. People I trust."

"And you trust me? You don't even know me."

"Don't I? I feel like I know enough. You're the kind of person you call when you need help."

The quiet of that stupid closet. His voice in the dark.

"I'm sorry," his world-famous voice said, and in the dark of the room that voice settled in a breathless place in her body. A lonely place full of cobwebs and broken dreams and heartache. "But...I kind of need you, Helen."

Well, it was going to take a seriously stronger woman than she was to resist Micah Sullivan saying he needed her.

She glanced at the clock in her room. Three a.m.

"I'll be there in a few hours."

"Thank you, Helen."

"You're..." She blinked. Shook her head. Wondered how everything had come to this. "You're welcome, Micah."

. . .

She finished getting dressed and made a travel mug of coffee before going up into her parents' room

"Hi, Mom, sorry," she said and crept to Mom's side of the bed. Mom woke up right away.

"Is everything okay? What's happening?" She pushed her silvery hair off her face, squinting at the clock, a red line from the pillow across her face.

"Everything is fine. Totally fine," Helen said quickly, deeply sorry she'd given her mom even a second to think the worst. They were too familiar with the worst, and Helen knew better. "You're not going to believe this," she said. "But I'm going to Rochester."

"Now? Why? Honey, what happened?"

"I'm picking up Micah Sullivan from jail." The words sounded totally ridiculous.

"The singer?" Mom asked after a second.

"What's going on?" Jonah said, rolling over to face them, blinking up at Helen. "Is everything all right?"

"Yes." She'd really screwed this up. "Everything is fine. I'm sorry. Actually…" Jonah would get a serious kick out of this. "I'm going to Rochester to pickup Micah Sullivan from jail."

Jonah looked like she'd smashed him upside the head with a frying pan. "The singer?" Helen nodded. "Wow."

"I know."

He pushed off the blankets. "Gimme a sec and I'll drive you—"

"No," she said and held out her hand, the keys to the truck dangling from her fingers. "I'm…going to do it. On my own."

Mom and Jonah had one of the silent conversations that they were so good at.

"You sure?" Jonah asked, lying back down in the bed. He put his hand on Daphne's shoulder and pulled her down, too, though she went stiff as a board.

"I'm sure. But Bea—"

"We've got Bea," Jonah said, still pulling Daphne down. They lay there like they'd never been in a bed before.

"Do you want a sandwich or something? For the road?" Daphne asked, unable to keep the worry out of her voice.

"Mom. I'm fine. I…got this," Helen said and then turned from her parents and walked out of the house to the truck in the driveway. The night was cool and clear, and she took a second to pull up directions to the Monroe County Jail, and another second to pull up a podcast, and then, with a deep breath, she pulled out of the driveway and onto the asphalt highway toward Micah.

CHAPTER
Eight

MICAH

The Monroe County Jail was, thank fuck, mostly empty. There was a drunk in the holding cell next to his who, after throwing what was a pretty good fit when he arrived, immediately passed out, pissed his pants and started snoring.

The cops, though, took their opportunity to walk by at more than regular intervals.

"If my people find a picture of this on social media," Micah said, his legs stretched out in front of him, "we'll hit you with a lawsuit so big you'll never work in law enforcement again." His arms were crossed over his chest. He'd been wearing a baseball cap, one of his favorites, but it had been taken from him at processing. He wished he had it now. It was hard work hiding under these impossibly bright lights.

The young cop who'd been pretending to look at his phone as he walked by, but was holding it at an angle that would imply he was taking a photo, nearly dropped the phone while shoving it back in his pocket.

"You know, you'd think a guy like you might figure out how

to stay out of jail," young cop said. Weird flex, but it wasn't new. Micah'd been getting this from cops since he was fifteen years old when his brother, at eight, shoplifted a remote control car that ended up being worth a stupid amount of money. When they got caught by the mall cops, Micah took the blame. It had escalated quickly and he was taken to the station in the back of a police car.

And being arrested that young, being handcuffed, being scared and vulnerable and alone–it was the worst.

But once the worst thing happened, it was over. And it wasn't the worst anymore. It was just a thing. And it was a thing that happened a lot.

Despite what his neighbor was able to accomplish, snoring away on the tiny bench, holding cells were no places to get some rest. The lights were bright and they buzzed real loud, and the ghosts of all a man's bad decisions sat right down next to him.

He could pace, try and burn out the anxiety, but he'd learned from hard experience that didn't work for him so well. He would only get more wound up. About his brother. About his own stupidity, letting it dictate shit even now.

I'm a grown-ass man. Alex is a grown-ass man. What am I doing?

The only thing for him to do was go deep in his head. And think about music.

But, for some reason, tonight it just wasn't working.

Because he'd called Helen.

Yep. He was locked out of his head because of a woman. And all he could think about was her. And wonder if he hadn't just made a huge mistake. He had a couple of handy reasons why he called her – reasons that weren't totally lies – the biggest one being that he needed to tell her. About the album. The songs.

"Sullivan?" The door swung open and the young cop stood there. "You've made bail. You're free to go."

It was just before six in the morning, which would mean that Helen had a lead foot and no problems on the highways.

Micah stood up, his knees creaking and his back sore from

resting against the cold concrete. He walked through the door and past the newbie, and felt the cop eyeballing him the whole way.

Micah grinned, his blood sizzling in that familiar way. *Try it,* he thought. *Just try it.*

But fresh new cop kept his cool and Micah walked out of the holding cell down a hallway, past processing and through another door that had to be buzzed open, and then he was in the main lobby of the Monroe County Jail.

And there was Helen.

She stood up from the chair where she'd been sitting and smiled at him awkwardly.

And all the bullshit reasons aside, he knew in his heart of hearts he called her because he wanted to see her again.

God. She was beautiful.

Her blond hair was pulled up onto the top of her head, bits of it falling down around her ears. She wore a green cotton skirt that came down to her knees and that denim jacket she'd worn the last time he saw her. Beneath it was a purple tank top that hugged her curves and her tight waist.

Part of surviving his childhood had been forgetting a lot of it. Some therapists had tried to convince him that just because his brain didn't remember, it didn't mean that his body didn't remember. Which, when he was younger, he'd thought was bullshit.

But he'd been brought to his knees lately with memory. With the way sunlight came through a dark curtain. The smell of bacon in the morning. The touch of an icy-cold hand on his wrist.

All that to say, when he looked at her, at Helen, he felt something. Something deep and profound and real in his body. He didn't know if was desire or memory or some powerful mix of the two, but he stood at dawn in the Monroe County Jail and felt weak at the sight of her.

He smiled and she smiled back, that cautious, careful smile that made him mad to know more about her.

But she wasn't alone. There were a dozen people standing in

the lobby. And it took no time for him to be recognized. One woman gasped and pushed her elbow into another woman's side. They started whispering.

Time to go, he thought.

"Hi," Helen said awkwardly, crossing the small hallway to him. "You okay?"

"Are you?" he asked, noting the dark circles under her eyes, which he knew were his fault. He wanted to feed her and tuck her into a bed immediately.

"Fine," she said, with a tired but real smile.

Behind her a guy was getting his phone out.

Fuck.

"Mr. Sullivan?" The sergeant stood behind the big desk with the plexiglass shield. He shoved a little plastic tray out through the slot and Micah grabbed his wallet, his phone and the cash he'd had in his pocket when he got arrested. His hat went immediately on his head like it had the power of protecting him now. But that cat was way out of the bag.

The sergeant held out a clipboard and Micah scrawled his signature across the bottom. Information about court dates and legal aid that would never really matter because Jo was so good at making this stuff go away.

"Thanks gentlemen," he said. "It's been a pleasure."

"Can we…ah…can we get a picture?" fresh new cop asked.

Oh man, he was too tired to fight it. And giving in to this stuff was the fastest way to make it go away.

"Sure," he said and they all stood together. Him, the sergeant and fresh new guy. Big smiles, peace signs flashed. The show complete.

"Hey! You that guy from the band?" Another person asked, phone already out and recording.

"I'm a guy from a band," he said with a smile he was far from meaning.

"Can I get an autograph?" the first woman asked, her friend recording the whole thing.

"Sure," he said, his feet firmly on the path of least resistance.

"What did you do, huh? To get arrested?" the guy asked again. Still recording.

"Got in a little dust-up," he said easily, though he was grinding his back teeth. "You know how it is."

He scrawled his name across a drugstore receipt the woman gave him.

"I love your music," she said in a quiet, nervous voice.

"Thank you. I appreciate that." He felt Helen watching all of this.

I wonder what she thinks?

"My friend dared me to do this," she said in a very quiet voice and handed him another receipt. "My number is on that. If, you know, you're ever in the neighborhood again." She gave him a little flirty look and pressed her breast against his hand in a way that looked accidental but totally wasn't.

"Hey, do you think you can call my sister?" new cop asked. "She's your biggest fan."

"Are you kidding me?" he asked the cop, his frustration leaking out.

"She'd lose her mind. Seriously."

"I'm not calling your sister."

"You don't have to be a dick about it."

He just wanted to leave.

"Hey," said the kid who didn't know him and was still recording everything. "Can you sing something?"

"No."

"I thought you were a singer. Sing something."

"Goodbye everyone." He lifted his arm, smiled as wide as he could and put his hand on Helen's back, guiding her toward the door.

"That your girlfriend?" the guy filming everything asked.

Micah jerked his hand away. "No," he said, turning back to the guy. "She's not."

And something about Micah's shift in energy told that guy all he needed to know. "Hey," he shouted at Helen. "What's your name? You this guy's girlfriend?"

"She's my driver," he said definitively, and then, like Helen was indeed his employee, he hit the door and walked out, letting her follow.

"Holy shit," she said, once they were out.

"Keep walking and don't look back." The guy would still be filming. "Which one is your car?"

"The…the black truck," she said, and then she must have hit her key fob and the lights blinked. He stepped sideways trying to block the license plate on the truck.

"Do I need to open your door or something?" she asked, and he liked that she was trying to make a joke.

"Just get us out of here."

In the rearview mirror he saw the kid with the camera, following them.

"We gotta go," he said. She started the truck and pulled out of the parking lot, tires squealing.

"Shit. I'm sorry," he said, looking behind them to see if anyone was getting into a car. It seemed like they'd all lost interest. "I shouldn't have—"

"Are you kidding?" she asked, her cheeks all flushed. She was smiling. "I feel like I just busted you out of jail. That's the most fun I've had in ages."

He laughed. "Well, we'll see if you're still laughing if that guy sells the footage to TMZ."

"Oh." She sobered. "That must be kind of a drag for you."

"You get used to it," he lied.

"People expect you to do all that for them? Call their sister and answer their personal questions? Sing on command?"

"Not all. But some, yeah."

"That must be hard."

"Well, let's not kid ourselves. There are harder things." He looked up at her under the curved bill of his baseball cap and waited for her to say something. To offer up what she knew of hard things.

Her lips tightened and that was it.

"White Plains?" she asked.

"How about some food first?"

"What?"

"I'm starving. You starving?"

"Sure…I…yes, I'm hungry."

"Excellent. I know just the place."

CHAPTER
Nine

HE TOOK her to Nick's on Main, which, because it was a weekday and now too late for the drunks and too early for the lunch crowd, they had pretty much all to themselves. She sat across from him at the scratched but immaculate Formica table and wrinkled her adorable nose, clearly trying to make sense of the menu.

"Don't bother," he said, flipping over their coffee mugs so the waitress could fill them. His mother would smack him upside the head if she'd still been around, but he kept his hat on. Sue him, he needed a little armor. "You can get all the usual breakfast things, but the thing you want is the garbage plate."

"I don't want anything called a garbage plate."

"I know. It feels counterintuitive, but in the end, you'll see."

"Decaf or regular?" The waitress asked, carrying a pot of each. He liked the looks of their waitress, nothing fazed her. She'd seen every kind of story unfold in these booths. He meant nothing to her.

"Regular," Helen said with a smile. "Cream, too, if you have it."

The waitress put a handful of creamers on the table in front of Helen. "You know what you want?" the waitress asked like she really couldn't give a shit. Micah loved it so much. He caught Helen smiling and loved that too.

"Garbage plates," he said.

"Fries or home fries."

"Home fries."

"Macaroni salad?"

"Of course."

"Cheeseburger, burger or Red Hots?"

He looked at Helen, trying to judge if she was a burger person or a hot dog person. "You're not vegetarian are you?" he asked, which for some reason made her howl with laughter.

"A little late for that," she said.

"One cheeseburger. One Red Hots," he answered. "With everything."

Their waitress grabbed the menus and left.

"Macaroni salad?"

"It's weird, I'll give you that. But the sweetness kind of rounds the whole thing out."

She made an unbelieving noise in her throat. "You'll see," he said, stretching out his legs. His knees bumped hers and they both recoiled too hard, too fast. "Everyone loves garbage plates in the end."

They fiddled with their coffee mugs. Adding milk and sugar and taking long sips and setting the cups down in just the right spot.

"Are you—"

"I should—"

They spoke at the same time and then laughed.

"Go ahead," he said.

"I was just going to ask you—what happened tonight?"

"Why I got arrested?"

She nodded and sipped her coffee.

"That is a long and complicated story." He gave her his most disarming grin, but she was not disarmed.

"Well, we've got a lot of time."

Right.

"My brother and I went into a bar, for a beer." He shrugged. "Some guy said something. My brother said something back. And here we are."

She blinked at him and then laughed. "Where is your brother?"

"Jo gave him a ride back to White Plains."

Her eyes went wide, and it reminded him so painfully of her at age fourteen that he had to look away. "But not you?"

"I was getting a ride in a cop car."

"So why didn't she stick around and bail you out? Or why didn't your brother?"

"You're getting mad on my behalf?" he asked, his lip curling in a smile. This was a rare treat.

"Someone should."

Quickly, he looked out the window, recovering from words that hit far too close to home, aware of her green-eyed gaze seeing more of him than he'd expected.

"I would think for a guy who gets in trouble a lot, you might have a body man or something."

"I used to, and I take umbrage to the phrase *a lot*. I get in trouble *some*. And a lot less than I used to. But it's hard to lie low when you've got a guy with no neck following you around wherever you go."

"So, there you are, lying low with your brother," she said. "A guy at a bar says something. Your brother says something back and you're the one arrested. Make it make sense, Micah."

"Well," he said, loving her smile. Loving the way she was all lit up on the other side of the booth. "First of all, my brother is fast. And he has no problem sacrificing me so he can get away. Once, when we were kids...well, he was a kid and I was old enough to know better, he ran his mouth off to, I swear, a hockey team. A good one. A big one. He says something about the goalie's mother and I am trying to keep the rest of the team from pummeling him into mush, when I hear him running. I look over my shoulder and he's a blur in the distance."

"Did they pummel you to mush?"

"No. Broke my nose," he touched the curved bridge of his nose. "I'm not as fast as my brother, but I was faster than those guys that day."

"And tonight? You're saying your brother ran away?"

"He doesn't actually run anymore. He slips away because a lot of people don't know who he is. He enjoys some relative peace and quiet with which to be mouthy. They get one look at me and a certain kind of asshole is, like, all right, I'm gonna get bragging rights forever."

"And you fight them?"

"That's the general idea."

"Why don't you walk away with your brother?"

"Have you ever been in a fight?" he asked, because she clearly didn't understand the rules.

"No! I mean…once. Sort of. This girl in middle school thought I kissed her boyfriend at a party and she stood up in home room and threw this note at me. And the worst part was that it got all tangled in my hair…and I had to, like, try and fish it out. It was embarrassing and everyone was staring. But the note said *Meet me after class. I'm going to kick your ass.*"

"Did she mean to rhyme?"

"I'm going to go with no."

"So, what?" he asked with a smile. "You didn't go after school and it just blew over?"

"No. I went. And I convinced her that I didn't kiss her boyfriend and that fighting people after school didn't really solve any problems."

"You're joking."

"I'm not. We actually became pretty good friends after that."

"That doesn't surprise me."

"So your brother starts stuff and you finish it? You're telling me that's how it went down?"

"Since we were kids."

"Why didn't Jo bail you out?"

"Because I think she is a little tired of our pattern and she thinks some tough love might break it."

"Will it?"

"It didn't tonight."

"I have never met anyone so comfortable with their self-destructive streak."

He spread out his arms. "I pride myself on being one of a kind."

This was one of the easiest most honest conversations he'd had with anyone outside of Danny in years. He knew when he had chemistry with someone, and the air between them fizzed and popped and he felt alive in this booth with her.

He'd spent some time after writing the album thinking about what it would be like to see her again. To spend time with her. He'd imagined she'd be wise and smart and kind.

But he'd never imagined the chemistry.

"So, how am I the lucky person to get the call from jail?"

He pulled his phone out of his back pocket, unlocked it and pushed it over to her.

"Have a look."

She glanced at him and then back down at the phone.

"Go ahead, honestly."

She tapped his contacts. There was a very short list.

"Jo. Alex, Sean, Miguel, Danny. You and my mom."

"You could have called your mom!"

"She died five years ago."

Her face fell in a way that could only be called funny. He laughed and she only looked more mortified. "I'm sorry. Why are you laughing?"

"You got a funny face."

She scowled at him and she was easily the cutest thing he'd seen in a lifetime.

"I keep her cell phone paid for and I call her number so I can listen to her message every once in a while."

"That's sweet."

"I was a bit of mama's boy."

"You wrote a whole song about it, didn't you?"

"Several."

"None of that explains why it's the band, your mother and me on your phone," she said. "And you called me!"

"I used to have everyone on my phone," he said. "Like, every contact I ever made. Every band I met at a party. Every hero I met at the Grammys. All of it. But since the lockdown, I decided to clean out my life a little bit. It all felt like distraction."

"Wow. I'm...I guess I just can't believe I made the cut." She laughed.

"Lucky for me," he said, with maybe a little too much earnestness. They'd been skirting flirtation, but he'd tipped them right into it and she stiffened, like she was suddenly seeing the chemistry too and didn't know what to make of it.

"Helen—" he started, about to come clean. Tell her that they'd met before and she'd left an impression on him, and he'd read the article and knew what happened to her fiancé and that none of this was an accident.

But their food arrived. And the moment was gone.

"Red Hots," the waitress said, putting down the plate with hotdogs, split in half and fired up on the grill. They were smothered with hot meat sauce, cheese and chopped onions. "And cheeseburger."

She put down the second plate of greasy, artery-clogging goodness.

Helen gaped at the food. "This is..."

"Amazing?"

"Repulsive?"

"Just try it."

"Which one is mine?" she asked.

"Whichever one you want."

She pulled the plate with the hot dogs closer to her.

"Really," he said. "I had you pegged as a cheeseburger girl."

"Hot dogs are a secret love of mine."

"Why secret?"

"Growing up on an organic fruit and vegetable farm, they were strictly outlawed."

"Which of course made you want them more?"

"Something like that," she said with a smile.

They unrolled their cutlery and slipped their paper napkins onto their laps.

She took a piece of home fry that was covered in meat sauce and cheese and a little of the macaroni salad dressing, and popped it into her mouth.

He watched her, knowing the inevitable end of this particular scene. He'd seen it too many times before. The garbage plate won over everyone it encountered.

"How do you know about this phenomenon?" she asked.

"I grew up in Rochester."

"I didn't know that," she said.

"You looking me up on line?" he asked, squinting at her. It would only be fair. After he read the article about her in the Times, he'd done a deep dive on all her social media. Looking for pictures of her like a creepy stalker.

She went for another bite and then another. The furrow between her eyes vanished. Her lips, shiny from grease, spread in an incredulous smile.

"It's good right?" he asked, digging into the cheeseburger.

"It's like a crime against humanity."

"But a delicious one."

She laughed and they ate in silence, and the instinct to tell her the truth went away.

"Have you ever tried that?" she asked.

"Crimes against humanity?"

"Talking the people who want to fight you out of fighting you?"

He narrowed his eyes at her. "What are you imagining that looks like?"

"Well, you know, you're rich. You're famous. People love your music."

"And I should pay my way out of a fight?"

"Or offer tickets or autographs. Or…" She trailed off, her eyes on his face. "No?"

"I would rather fight than do that," he said.

"Why?"

He didn't know how to put into words that his music was him. And fighting was more about his brother and his childhood, so it was easier to fight. How did he explain that fighting cost him nothing. Nothing that mattered.

"I don't know how to answer that," he said, honestly.

She looked up at him through her lashes and the edge of her bangs, and he was struck by a lightning bolt of lust. Something so real and so visceral he needed a second to get hold of himself.

Her eyes were green, a real dark green. The color of a lake. And the freckles. The freckles slayed him. Ruined him. He lost track of his thoughts, looking at the freckles across her cheeks and scattered across her chest where the low neck of her cotton camisole revealed them.

It had been ages since he'd felt this way. Longer than anyone would believe. Longer than he could admit and still keep his rock-and-roll credibility.

Which was why, he guessed, she hit him this way. Like a fist just below his belly button. Deep into his body. A solid throb. A deep ache.

She coughed, glancing back down at their food, and he realized all these things he was feeling, she was feeling, too. And it felt like they were on a high wire together, the whole rest of the world a distant blur.

He could get drunk on this feeling.

"You know what would make this garbage plate better?" she

asked, changing the subject. She licked her lips, leaving them damp and lush.

"Nothing. Not one single thing. It's perfection on a plate," he said.

"Sour cream and salsa."

He wanted to take one finger and trace the edge of that purple camisole and he wanted to exert the slightest pressure against it, pushing it back. Out of his way. So he could see more of her skin, the freckles, the top curves of her breasts.

"Micah?"

"Let's see if you're right," he said, snapping back into his body. He lifted his hand and asked the waitress for sour cream and salsa, which arrived in little plastic ramekins.

"My god," he said, after swallowing a bite. "I did not think garbage plates could be improved upon, but you have done it. You are a wonder, Helen."

She laughed, her cheeks going pink. And he bent over his food, distracting himself.

After a few minutes, she pushed her plate away, still more than half full. "I cannot eat any more."

"Yeah," he said. "I'm out, too. Finishing a garbage plate is a rookie mistake."

"The heartburn alone is gonna kill you."

He laughed. "I think when you're young and drunk—"

"Beer soaks it all up. Makes sense."

He put some cash on the table. "Hey," he said, suddenly realizing he owed her what might be a thousand dollars. "The bail."

"You know, we're going to add it to what you're contributing to Haven House."

"All right."

"But you're going to double it."

"You are ruthless, Helen."

"For Haven House, yes," she said with a definitive nod. "Someone needs to be ruthless for those women."

Inspiration, for him, struck out of the blue. The lightning bolt of hearing something. Of connecting a feeling to a word. A chord to a progression. He could do all the shit that creative coaches told a person to do—set the stage for creativity, sit down every day at the same time, practice writing garbage.

But it was total bullshit.

The good stuff came in a lightning bolt. There was no other way.

"Micah?" she asked.

"Yeah." He patted down his pockets. "You got a pen?"

"Sure," she said in the tone of voice of a person who had supplies for a lot of emergencies. She put a big leather purse on the table and fished out a pen.

He wanted to ask her what else she had in there, but he couldn't look away from what was happening in his head. If he did, it might vanish.

He started to scribble on the back of the napkin and she watched him for a while and he was about to be self-conscious when she finally asked, quietly, "Can you walk to the car and write?"

"Yep," he said, and scooted out of the booth and kept scribbling away on the napkin.

He followed her to her truck, got in the passenger seat, and before they were at the highway, he had the first verse and the bridge of what he thought was a pretty great song. He tucked the napkin into his pocket and put the pen down in the console between them.

"So?" she said, a twinkle in her eye. "Did I just watch a hit song get written?"

"You watched something get written, hard to say what it is yet."

"Wow." She glanced over at him, smiling. "That was...that was really cool."

"Glad I could entertain you."

"Now, White Plains?" she asked and then yawned so big her jaw practically cracked.

"How about I drive?" he asked, and she jerked her head to look at him so fast he wondered if he'd accidentally said "How about I fuck you in the backseat."

"Sorry," she said. "I mean…maybe. I don't…"

He was making her nervous and he didn't know what he'd said or done, but it was obviously an issue with the car.

"I can drive," he said. "I have a license. And it's valid."

"No. I mean, I'm sure you can. It's just… " She closed her eyes and blew out a long breath. "I have a control thing. Around cars."

"In that you like them to be controlled?"

She laughed a little, which was the point.

"You gonna tell me about it?" he asked.

She looked out over the steering wheel. It was going to be a gray day, too many clouds. He knew, of course, why she didn't like driving. Or he could guess—it didn't take a genius to figure it out. But he didn't want to tell her that he knew. That instinct in the diner to come clean was gone. And now he wanted her to trust him with the information.

Let me in, Helen. The way I let you in.

CHAPTER

Ten

"I USED to drive all the time. I loved it. I still love it." She gave him a shy smile and he tried to control his breathing. "But my fiancé was killed in a car accident."

She made a sound like a laugh, but wasn't a laugh. Not at all. She clapped her hand over her mouth.

"Hey. I'm sorry," he said with sincerity. "We don't have to talk about it."

"It's okay. It's just…" She pulled in a breath and held it. Held it for far too long. He touched her shoulder and she let her breath go with a giant exhale. "I don't talk about him. You know. I don't… " She pressed her lips together. "I live with people who know what happened and they never talk about him. So, I don't. That's weird, isn't it?"

She looked at him like she wanted confirmation on the weirdness of all of it.

"You can talk about him if you want," he said. "Or not. No pressure from me."

"I was pregnant with Bea. And it was Christmas three years ago. And he was killed in a car accident."

"Were you with him?" His heart spiked at the thought.

"No. He was hit by a tractor trailer that lost control in a storm.

He died right away. Which you know is one of those truly horrific things that is also a blessing."

"Yeah." He'd had a few of those things in his life, too.

"The police found the driver hadn't had any real bad weather training. She didn't pull over when she should have. And it was one thing when he died in this terrible accident, but suddenly it wasn't just an accident, and the driver of the truck was going to jail and I was supposed to sue the trucking company."

"You didn't."

He knew all this. And he wanted her to trust him, but now he felt like the world's biggest asshole. Pretending not to know, basically lying, while she bared her soul to him.

He'd read her story and it had changed him, and now he could never say that.

The problem with lies. Even lies by omission. They were always a trap.

Fuck.

"No," she said. "By the time the trial had rolled around, I had a newborn and I just wanted to move on and...I don't know. Try and protect myself." She shrugged. "I might have gone a little too far with that idea." She gave him a self-deprecating smile.

"What did you do?" he asked, though he knew.

"The trial was over Zoom, and I read a victim's statement and I basically forgave her. Putting her in jail or suing the company wouldn't bring back Evan. It couldn't make me feel better and it couldn't make her feel worse. She was...I mean, she was in so much pain, and I just saw it and wanted to make it better in a way. So that's what I did."

"Did you mean it?"

She gave him a slightly startled look. "No one ever asks me that."

He thought of her question about why it was easier to fight than offer up some part of his music and he felt the fizz and pop of their chemistry again. The way she saw him, and he saw her, wasn't the way the world saw them. It was special.

"You don't have to answer."

"I've been thinking lately that maybe I didn't." She sounded so pained and he couldn't stand it. He put his hand on her shoulder again, cupping the muscle and bone with his palm. She was warm and strong. "Or that maybe forgiveness is something I have to choose every day. Practice. Every day. Because...she writes me. From jail."

"Really?"

"I don't read the letters," she said. "I tear them up and throw them away, and I think if I really forgave her I'd be able to read them."

"I don't know," he said. "Maybe it's your way of moving on. Those letters just keep the wound fresh."

"Do you think?" she asked. "Really?"

"I think, really."

Her smile was luminous. Honestly, so beautiful.

Fuck. He felt his body buzz. His brain flooded with images and ideas and he reached into his pocket for the pen she gave him and the napkin.

But then he stopped himself. He'd used enough of her pain as inspiration without her ever knowing it.

"Sorry," she said with a laugh. "I really unloaded on you there. Between the accident and then the pandemic and having a baby, I just haven't done a whole lot of driving. So you calling me to come get you is kind of awesome, really. Pulled me right out of my comfort zone."

"Well, our situation hasn't changed. Someone has to drive us, and you're clearly exhausted."

"I am. Aren't you, though?" she asked. "I mean, did you sleep at all last night?"

"No. I didn't..."

"Then I should drive."

"Well, I think the point I'm making is that neither of us should drive."

"We could get a few hours sleep at a rest stop," she said. "I used to do that all the time when I was driving home from school."

He started shaking his head the second she said *rest stop.* "Helen, we can skip sleeping on the side of the road and we can also get a few hours' sleep at a hotel."

"Are you a snob? Too good to sleep at a rest stop?" She was teasing him and he loved it. No one teased him. They thought he was too serious or cool or some shit. But here she was, so tired she was punch drunk, and teasing him.

"No. I've done it plenty. Too much. So, I know it's total garbage. Don't try and make it like I'm the strange one here," he teased her back and pulled out his phone. With the last of his battery, he found the nearest hotel and got them two rooms. "Come on. A couple hours sleep and a shower is just ten miles north."

"That's the wrong direction," she said.

"Helen, please don't take this the wrong way, but at this point, I do not care."

"No," she said. "Me neither. A few hours' sleep sounds good."

The sun was a bright yellow ball, struggling through the clouds just over the horizon and she turned north, following the directions on his phone and soon they were at a nothing special highway hotel.

"Okay, we're checked in," he told her, having done it over the phone. "I've given your name. You need to go get the keys."

"I do?"

"I mean, I can, but the risk of there being some kind of scene gets exponentially higher."

"No," she said. "I'm too tired for scenes. I'll get the keys." She turned to him, with a different kind of look in her eye. "But it's going to cost you."

If she was any other woman, he could assume she was propositioning him and his dick. Well, his dick quite liked that scenario. His dick was invested in paying off his debt to this lady the good old-fashioned way.

He smiled at her.

She blinked and her mouth fell open. "No. Not like…not like that."

"I didn't say anything."

"You didn't have to. Your dirty mind was broadcasting it loud and clear."

"What is all of this going to cost me?" he asked. "Besides double the cost of my bail, the cost of breakfast and a few hours at chez Holiday Inn."

"The fundraiser also has two auctions. A silent auction and…a bachelor auction."

"I'm sorry, what now?"

"It's not all bachelors and it's not at all dirty. Guys volunteer to build tree houses and do repair work around a house. Clean gutters. The fire chief volunteers a week's worth of home-cooked meals. It's actually very wholesome."

"I am not wholesome."

"What if you volunteered an hour-long private concert?"

He blinked at her, mouth open. "Do you have any idea how much I get paid to do that?"

"Like…a lot?"

"Like a lot."

"How about an hour-long music lesson?"

"How about no."

"Okay, what can you donate to the silent auction?"

"Besides a bunch of cash?"

"You got more of those napkins?" she asked, twirling her finger at him. "With bits of songs on them?"

"You're kidding me." His mouth fell open—he was stunned and delighted by her balls. "You want my historical song-writing documents."

"I want a little bit of that magic I got to watch happen in real life. I want a little bit of the reality behind the albums and the photos and the slick stage show."

"My soul, then?" he said quietly, staring into those green eyes of hers.

"Just a tiny bit," she said, holding her fingers about an inch apart.

"You know," he said, "there are women who would pay me for a night at the…" He looked out the window. "Holiday Inn."

"I'm sure there are. I am not one of them."

Suddenly another lightning bolt, this one to his already invested dick. He wondered what it would take to get her to the point that she *was* one of them. What would it be like to have Helen take what she was owed? From him? What would it be like to be used by Helen?

Good, he imagined. All that earnestness and focus. The fucking honesty.

His brother was wondering what was wrong with him since the pandemic and this was it—he couldn't take the bullshit anymore. He craved something real. Authentic.

He craved Helen.

He cleared his throat and looked away from her profile, trying to get a grip.

"I've got tons of napkins and receipts and even a notebook I used during the pandemic," he told her. But he didn't tell her that every word had been about her.

"We can have it?"

"You can have it."

And then, like he'd willed it into happening, she smiled, breathtaking and sincere, and she put her hand over his. Her fingers kind of circling his wrist. Her skin against his. Her fingertips on the tender bits, on the inside, where his pulse beat so close to the surface.

In his past, as a young rock star, he'd had a taste of everything the world had heard about. Groupies and orgies and constant, endless one-night stands with adoring women who loved his music and sucked his dick, then vanished when it was over like it never really happened.

He'd tasted every bit of that low-hanging fruit until it was rotten in his hands. In his mouth.

But Helen…her touch on his skin. Her smile.

It wasn't an invitation for him to lean forward, to press his mouth to hers. To taste her. He knew that, and he was leaning forward anyway.

She jerked her hand back, blinking at him.

"Helen," he breathed. "I'm…

"I'll go get our keys," she said and got out of that truck fast.

"Nice one, Micah," he said into the silence of her truck "Fucking nice one."

CHAPTER
Eleven

Helen

That was not what it looked like. I mean…there just wasn't any way that was what it looked like.

Helen pressed the little buzzer at the front desk and waited for someone to come and give her the keys. She waited and she told herself she was exhausted, severely out of practice and completely delusional.

"There's no way he was going to kiss me," she whispered.

"I'm sorry?"

Right. Now she was talking to herself. She took a deep breath and smiled at the young man behind the desk who looked like the buzzer had woken him up from a nap.

She told him her name, got the keys and braced herself to go back out and face Micah again. He was out of the truck, leaning against the tailgate, his hat pulled down low.

Even if you couldn't see his face, you knew there was something about him. Long legs. The boots. The aura. You'd take another look at him without even knowing who he was.

He looked like *someone*. And she was no one.

He wasn't going to kiss you. You were being delusional.

Right. That was the only thing that made sense. So she committed to it fully. Took a deep breath and pulled down the edge of her denim coat. "Got the keys," she said. "We're on the second floor."

"Great."

"It's weird going to a hotel without any luggage," she said, making awkward small talk as they crossed the parking lot. It was awful to be so strained with a guy she'd literally bared her soul to. But that was her current superpower—making shit awkward.

The trees behind them were full of birds, and between their noise and the highway she was actually shouting her small talk.

The awkwardness was too much.

"I haven't carried my own luggage into a hotel in years," he said.

See, she thought. *See how ridiculous it would be to think he was going to kiss you? He doesn't even carry luggage.*

At the side entrance, he held out his hand and she gave him the keys. Careful there was no accidental skin touching.

Oh, she realized. That's...maybe he was going to kiss her because she'd basically reached over and held his hand. It was flimsy. But women probably did that sort of thing to him all the time. Maybe *he* thought *she* was going to kiss *him*. And was just responding in kind.

"All right," he said, in front of their doors. Their rooms were across the hall from each other. "Here." He handed her one key and she turned to open her door. "I'll see you in a few hours," he said.

"Wait!" The word blurted out of her mouth and she closed her eyes and swore at herself.

"Yeah?" he asked. She turned back to him, stunned all over again, by how...god, handsome wasn't the right word. It wasn't even close to the right word. How *real* he was. How...profoundly present he was. He took up the right amount of space for a man. The right amount of air, but still there seemed to be more weight to him. More…life. That was it. Even exhausted from a night spent in jail he just seemed more alive than other people.

"Helen?"

"I wasn't coming on to you, in the car," she said. Blurted. Again. She was real blurty right now. "I mean, it might have seemed that way." She did this spastic kind of reenactment of grabbing his wrist. "But I wasn't, because that would be ridiculous, you know? Me hitting on you. I'm, like, a single mom, did I tell you that? I am. Not that single moms aren't…like, sexual creatures. I'd say more so, you know? Because we remember and miss…things." *Oh my god, oh my god, shut up, Helen. Shut up.*

"Anyhoo, I don't want things to be weird because you think I was going all…what are you doing?" she asked as he stepped away from his door and closer to her. She moved back and the hallway was small, so one more step back and she was pressed flat against her door. He put his hand on the doorframe near her head, all the veins and muscles in his forearm standing out against his skin, and this was the most sexual thing that had happened to her in *years.*

The air between them was smoke and fire, and her eyes were about to cross with sudden-onset horniness.

He wasn't even touching her, but it felt like he was pushing her up against that door.

He wasn't even touching her and she was wet.

"Nothing about you is ridiculous," he whispered. His breath was against her lips and her eyelids fought a humongous fight to stay open. Her knees were working hard too, keeping her upright. Really, this was just a full-frontal attack on her whole body. Her lungs were going to stop working any second.

"You can hit on me anytime," he whispered. "And if there are…things you miss, I'd be happy to remind you." And then, he just stood there. So close she could smell him, coffee and fried food from the diner, and beneath that something citrusy. Him. His skin was the citrusy stuff. Her fingers twitched and she realized how badly she wanted to touch him.

That sweet soft bit of skin just outside the collar of his shirt. He wore necklaces, one on a chain, the other on a bit or rawhide, and both of them crisscrossed that terrain. It was where his heart was beating and it the skin looked so soft, like velvet, and it would take nothing, absolutely nothing to rise up on her tiptoes and press her lips to that skin.

It would be warm, she thought. He would be warm.

And parts of her had been cold, dropped in ice cold, Han Solo in the carbonite cold, for over three years.

"Helen?" he breathed, like he wasn't sure what she was thinking, like he'd finally clued in that this wasn't a normal reaction to a rock and roll sex god by a twenty-nine-year-old single mother. That something else was going on and she couldn't take it anymore.

She couldn't even say anything to make her exit graceful. She couldn't even laugh or make a joke. Her entire self was going haywire.

It was rude. But she couldn't take it anymore and she turned away from him, her shoulder hitting his chest. Brushing against it until he stepped back, but too late. Her skin registered the feel of his body against hers and was currently extrapolating that all over her body. Stupid body.

She fumbled with the key, once, twice, realized she had it upside down.

"Helen."

"Good night!" she cried, and thank the lord the key was right and she got the door open and nearly fell into the dark sanctuary of her room. The door slammed shut between them, leaving Micah Sullivan standing in the hallway.

She was tired, yes. But now she was absolutely ruined with adrenaline. She took off her clothes, crawled into bed, pulled the blankets up over her head and called Josie.

"Helen!" Josie answered on the second ring. "What are you doing—"

"You have to help me."

"Are you okay? Is Bea okay?" Her cousin/best friend's voice got sharp.

"She's fine…but Josie." She closed her eyes, not even sure how she was going to get the words out. "Josie."

"You are officially freaking me out."

"I almost kissed Micah Sullivan."

"What?"

"Or…he almost kissed me. It's all kind of a blur right now."

"Helen. You need to start at the beginning."

It took five minutes to catch Josie up to speed, especially since she got very distracted by the part of the story that took place in the closet.

"You asked him if he was going to pee?"

"Not my finest moment, Jos. But also—not the point."

When she was done, she waited for her cousin's wise words of wisdom to fill her with guidance.

"Jesus, Helen. What are you going to do?" Josie asked.

"Ummm. That's why I'm calling you."

"Well, if you want my opinion I think you should get off the phone with me and go knock on that guy's door and get naked."

"I can't."

"Why?"

Helen opened her mouth and shut it. It was too humid under the blankets and she tore them off, but still didn't have a reasonable answer.

"Because of Evan?" Josie asked.

"No," she said. "Evan would…I mean, this sounds crazy. But Evan would want me to …*you know* with Micah Sullivan."

"Okay, if you're going to call it *you know*, you're not ready."

"That's what I'm saying, Josie. I'm not ready. I was with Evan for years and before him it was…god, that football player in high school and then the guy who worked at the library with me first year of college. Like, I'm never going to be ready for Micah Sullivan."

Josie made a quiet noise. That sounded like understanding and also pity.

Helen stiffened. "You know, never mind, it's probably late where you are—"

"We're in New York City," she said. "It's barely eight in the morning."

"I'm not pitiful."

"You aren't. And I think…well, I think if you let this opportunity slide by you, you will regret it for, like, ever. And there has to be a first person after Evan, and I don't know, why not let that first person be a rock god? He'll be good at it. I think that's a given."

There was a mumble of another voice.

"Cameron says hi," Josie said.

"Okay, but don't—"

"Do you think Micah Sullivan will be good in bed?" Josie asked Cameron. There was a laugh and a mutter. "Cameron says he thinks, yes. He'll be good in bed."

All this talk of being good in bed was making her a little queasy. Or maybe that was the garbage plate.

"All right," Helen whispered, the adrenaline from nearly kissing Micah having worked off, leaving her even more tired than before. She felt herself melting into the mattress. Exhaustion coming for her. "I'm going to bed."

"Okay," Josie said. "But remember, you deserve to be happy. And Evan would want you to be happy and life keeps going, Helen. It keeps going."

Micah

Calling his brother was a mistake. But calling his mother wasn't an option anymore, so the only person he really had was his brother. And he didn't want to fight. He wanted to fuck Helen

Larson against a hotel door. But since *that* wasn't an option, either, fighting with his brother was all he had.

"Holy shit," Alex said on the first ring. "You got picked up."

"Yes, I got picked up, you asshole."

"Why didn't you call me to come get you?"

"Like you would have come, you were out of that bar so fast, Alex."

"Yeah, did you see the size of those guys? Shit. I can't believe you stayed."

"Someone has to stay, Alex. Someone has to take responsibility."

"Jesus, listen to yourself, Micah. It's a fight not a bar bill. And those fuckers started it."

Micah squeezed the bridge of his nose, exhaustion giving him a headache.

"Tell Jo I'll be back in White Plains in a few days."

"Taking time to see the sights of Rochester?" Alex laughed. "So, who'd you call to get you?"

He didn't want to say. And that he didn't say was already too much of an answer.

"Danny peddled his bike out to ride you bitch?"

"Don't..." he sighed. "Leave the kid alone."

"Who'd you call?" Alex asked like it was all a joke. Like the hundreds of times in his life Alex had left with some girl or some cooler guy and abandoned Micah to sort his own way home. Once, memorably, at a party on a boat. His brother had left on another boat.

"Helen."

"Helen? Who the fuck is...the charity girl?"

"Her name is Helen Larson."

"She's, like, three hours away. And you called her? And she came?" Alex started to laugh. "Remember that wrong number you called, and it was some girl in Australia and she flew all the way—"

"I remember."

"She flew all the way to Seattle to fuck you."

And he'd fucked her because that was what he did.

"Alex. It's not like that."

"Then what's it like?"

Again. More silence and the thing with Alex was, if you gave him silence he'd fill it. "You have a thing for her?"

"You sound like an idiot."

"You *like*, like her?" He said it in a singsong voice and Micah was filled, as ever, with the joint urges to laugh and put his fist through his brother's face.

"So why are you calling? Just to talk about your feelings?"

There were suddenly twenty questions he wanted to ask his brother. Did he mean to start those fights and then bail? Did he mean for Micah to get hurt? What urge was this bullshit satisfying for Alex? But instead, he did what he always did when he felt this way. Turned inside out and upside down, wishing, god, just wishing for a soft place to land.

Shit. He pulled the napkin out of his pocket and wrote that down.

"No, I called to give you shit about leaving me in that bar."

"Look," Alex said. "I'm sorry about that fight. That guy was just such an asshole, talking shit about the band."

"There's always someone who is going to talk shit about the band," Micah said.

"Fine, but they're not going to do it to my face. Look at what we've done. What we're doing. Opening Madison Square Garden in September."

Right. Because this was the truth. It wasn't just the past they had, it was the future. And everything Micah had ever dreamed of came true with Alex.

Those were the real ties that bound them together. Not just the promise he made to mom. But the promise they made to each other every time they walked on stage together as Band of Outlaws.

"Right," he said, reminded of what was important. "Madison Square Garden."

"Hey," Alex said. "About Danny."

"You went, right?" Micah took a deep breath, still pissed about what Alex had said to Danny. The kid didn't deserve that shit. And the whole point of this trip had been for Alex to go up and apologize to Danny.

"No. Actually."

"Alex!"

"Look, I mean it. The kid doesn't belong in the band. I know Sean agrees."

"No, he doesn't."

"Have you asked him? Really asked him?"

Yes. Of course. *Probably.*

"This is bullshit, Alex."

"Look, I'll apologize to the guy, but the bigger issue is that he shouldn't be in the band. You know it. All of us know it."

"So who plays bass?"

"Miguel—"

"Miguel can't walk up a flight of stairs without needing a break." He'd gotten COVID at the very beginning and was still getting his strength back.

"That's not true anymore," Alex said.

"How do you know?" Micah demanded.

"I talked to Sandra."

"You called his wife?"

"Yeah, and he's doing better. He's exercising. She said his lungs are functional. He gets tired, but the tour is still months away. He can come next week to rehearsals."

It all made sense, suddenly. What Alex said to Danny, and then agreeing to come up here so he could apologize, only to predictably get in a fight and bail on him. *God, why didn't I see this coming?* "You planned this. You got all this in order and then you said that shit to Danny."

"You're not the only one who takes care of the band, Micah. In fact, I'd go so far as to say, I'm the one protecting it from you, right now."

"The fuck—"

"Band votes. You know that. Talk to Sean."

Alex hung up and Micah swore. Loudly.

And then he texted Sean.

Be honest. Danny? Yes or no?

Sorry mate, the answer came back immediately. *But it's no. He's a sweet kid and the road will eat him up.*

Fuck. Just…fuck.

CHAPTER

Twelve

Helen

She woke up to the buzz of her phone. One quick buzz, which meant an incoming text. Really bad stuff didn't come in as a text.

Eyes still shut she reached out from the cocoon of blankets she'd absolutely fallen into after talking to Josie and grabbed her phone.

Coffee?

The text was from Micah. He must have walked to a coffee shop.

Yes. Please. Lots of milk. No sugar.

He sent back a thumbs-up.

She rubbed the sleep from her eyes and called her mom real quick.

"Hi honey," Mom said when she answered. "How are you doing?"

"Fine. I'm just getting up." Before falling asleep, she'd texted her mom saying it would be a few more hours.

"That was smart not driving when you're tired."

Helen chuckled. Yes. It was. But sometimes she thought Mom

might say anything she did was smart. They'd fallen into some weird coping mechanisms the last few years.

"How is Bea?"

"How is Bea every day?" Mom asked, her voice radiating joy and love.

"Covered in jam and bossy?" Helen said.

"Well, that, but she's also a delight. She's watching a cartoon while I get her dinner."

"I should be home…I don't know…" She tried to do the math, but without coffee it was very difficult to add numbers.

"Don't worry, honey. She's fine. We're fine. Take as much time as you need."

"Well, I shouldn't need more than today. I'm hoping to be back tonight."

"So…" Mom dropped her voice. "How is he?"

Smart. Funny. Mercurial. Difficult. Kind.

"He's nice, Mom."

"Nice like what?"

Helen laughed. "What does that mean?"

"Nice like a hot cup of coffee. Or nice like…you know, sex."

Helen sighed. Both, she thought. He's nice like both. But she wasn't about to tell her mother that.

"Goodbye mom. Kiss Bea for me."

"I will. Oh, hey, Jonah is, like, obsessed with finding out how Micah heard about Haven House. Find out, would you? And then text him so I'm not hearing about it all the time."

"I will, Mom." There was a knock on her door and she felt her heart spike. Her face flush. Just knowing he was there, outside the door, made her feel…*buzzy.* "I need to go, Mom, we're getting on the road."

Mom hung up and Helen kicked off the blankets, put on her clothes, took one look at herself in the mirror and thought…well, there's not much I can do about that. And opened the door.

Micah Sullivan leaned against the doorframe with his baseball cap pulled down low. He wore a flannel shirt over an old faded gray shirt, the lettering all but worn off. His jeans…his jeans were nearly indecent. Worn and kind of crumpled, it was like they were hugging his junk.

And now she was… staring at his junk.

He held out a to-go cup of coffee and grinned at her. Like he knew, of course he knew.

"Milk no sugar," he said.

"There's a coffee shop around here?"

"I had it delivered."

"That's the most decadent thing I have ever heard in my life."

He laughed. "Honey, you need to get out more."

They agreed to meet out at the car in fifteen minutes.

"Here. I had this delivered, too." He picked up a plastic bag at his feet and handed it to her. Inside was deodorant, toothpaste and a toothbrush.

"Oh my god, you ordered me underwear?"

"From Walmart," he said, turning back around toward his door. "Don't get too excited."

Well, joke was on him. All her underwear came from Walmart.

"But you don't have to buy me stuff—"

"It's just money, Helen," he said. "And I've got a lot of it."

And then he was back behind his door and she was left, mouth-gaping, staring into an empty hallway.

She took a shower, used everything he'd bought her, guzzled her coffee and was outside at the truck in fifteen minutes. He came sauntering out a few minutes late.

Yeah. He sauntered. There was no other word for it.

He crossed the parking lot like it was a stage and people were screaming his name.

It was hot.

"You ready?" she asked and they both climbed into the car. She started to set up her phone's navigation for White Plains and he put his hand over hers.

Fuck, she thought, trying to play it cool. Part of her wanted to tell him to take it easy on her with this stuff. This casual touching, flirtation thing. She was like a puppet with too many strings and too many joints. She had no control and every twitch felt like it sent her jerking all over the place.

But she also didn't know how to interpret it. He was Micah Sullivan and he was flirting with her, and he did that as easily as he breathed. She didn't even know how to receive it. He touched her hand and she wanted to shriek with laughter, like he'd tickled her.

"Quick favor," he said.

She narrowed her eyes at him.

He opened his mouth, shut it and then smiled. "Has anyone ever told you, you are adorable when you're angry."

"Has anyone ever told you you're not as charming as you think you are?"

He gasped, clutched his hand to his chest. "My god, woman. You're vicious."

And he was ridiculous. And charming. Very, exceedingly charming.

"What's your favor?"

"My bass player, Danny, lives up this way and I need to go see him. Honestly, it should only be an hour detour."

"You know I have a daughter, right? A child who calls me Mommy and hasn't seen me for a day."

He made a chagrined face. "Right. Of course. I forgot about your daughter. Sorry—"

"I will take you to Danny's," she said, once he seemed to feel guilty enough. "But it will cost you."

"What more could you possibly want from me?" he asked, denim-blue eyes bright.

So much. Remind me what it feels like to be touched by a man. To be desired. Remind me what it feels like to be out of my head. To be sweaty and crazy. Remind me what sex feels like. And come tastes like.

Holy shit, what is wrong with me?

"Whatcha thinking about over there, Helen?" he asked, his lips twisted in a smile.

His eyes hot.

"You're going to play at the picnic," she blurted.

"What?" He laughed. "You know I'm kicking off a gigantic world tour at Madison Square Garden literally that same month."

"Two days before, actually."

"And you want me to sing in a park?"

"This is my demand. You want a ride? Doesn't come for free."

"So, I give you thousands of dollars, am donating all my song-writing stuff and now you want me to play the picnic? How about a signed guitar?"

"I'll take that, too."

He gasped at her and she laughed with delight. He really was so charming.

"You're a mercenary, Helen Larson."

"Twenty-minute set. You let us advertise. I can provide transportation back and forth. We're literally right up the road."

"Can I think about it?"

"Sure." She unrolled her window and took the key out of the ignition, humming like she had all the time in the world.

"You," he said, "are a real piece of work."

"I've been told."

"By who?"

"My…" She stopped, realized the words at the tip of her tongue had not been said in a while. "Fiancé."

"Is this a…current fiancé?" he asked, like he'd been thinking about that little scene in front of her hotel room door the way she had. And her being engaged changed the whole nature of that moment.

"No. The man who died. I'm not…there hasn't been anyone else."

Ugh. Helen, too far. Too much.

"I'm sorry, Helen," Micah said, his familiar rock-star voice gruff with pity. She shook her head, squared her shoulders. She fucking hated pity.

"Stop staring," she said, glancing over at him. He shook his head and she laughed, stunned by his audacity.

"You won't stop staring?"

He shrugged. "I can't."

"Because you feel bad for me?"

"Because my driver is beautiful."

"Oh my god," she cried, choosing to laugh at his words, to not take them seriously, because taking them seriously would fuck her up. "You're a terrible flirt."

"I'm great at it, actually. But I agree to your outrageous demands. I will play at your picnic."

"I knew you'd see it my way. Punch the new address into my phone," she said, eyes back on the road. Her hands at ten and two. Under total control.

The highway, and the way home, and the farm and the inn, her family, her daughter, they were all to the left.

The navigation told her to turn right, away from everything familiar. Into the unknown.

And weirdly, she was excited.

MICAH

Jesus Christ, man, you gotta tell her what you know about her.

At the very least he needed to stop pretending he didn't know *anything* about her. The truth was going to come out that they'd met when they were kids and that he'd read that *New York Times* article and he was going to look like an asshole and she was going to be pissed that he'd lied.

The silence in the car pounded with opportunity for him to tell the fucking truth.

A little bit, you saved my life. Twice. And I've spent the last month looking you up on facebook and staring at that picture of you in the yellow sweater. I am consumed by you and you don't know it.

"You comfortable?" she asked, reaching forward for the vent, turning it away from her.

"Fine," he said.

"So, how are rehearsals going?" she asked. "Is it like riding a bike?"

"In a lot of ways, yes," he said. "But we've had a lot of time off and our bass player got pretty sick, so right now it's like riding a bike with two flat tires."

She glanced over at him, smiling, like he was just so clever.

And that was why he didn't tell her. Because he liked the way she looked at him.

And he really fucking liked looking at her.

She drove with both hands on the wheel, but the hem of her skirt was hiked halfway up her thigh, and he was mesmerized by the freckles on her knees.

And last night, in front of her door, he'd wanted to kiss her. Suck that fragile skin on her neck. The pretty pink bow of her upper lip. He wanted to wrap his hands in her hair, make her gasp. Stroke her until she calmed down. Until she was used to him. Until she was rising to meet his touch, turning toward him for more. He wanted to stroke her until she came, trembling under his hand.

He wanted this beautiful woman undone. Her mysteries revealed.

And if he told her that would never happen.

Jesus. I'm an asshole.

The sun was setting hard in the west and the shadows across the highway were long. Golden-hour light, and it hit her cheeks and her eyes, turning that deep green to something light and golden.

After that nap, and some coffee, maybe it was the pretty light but there was something different about her. Or maybe he was just growing used to her, seeing past the first layer of cute and a little damaged. To all that subtle strength and devious humor.

Or maybe what he was seeing was the reality of her, past what he'd built up in his head after reading that article.

It was tricky, seeing and meeting and spending time with a muse. Who didn't know she was a muse.

She'd turned the radio to a pop station, that was playing the top requested songs of the week.

"Coming in for the first week since it's release and going

straight to the top of chart – This is Forgiveness by Band of Outlaws."

"Hey!" She said. "That's you!"

The steady pound of the drums. And then the bass. Like a dirge at the beginning, gathering steam and strength, until it was a late-night kitchen dance party by the end. It was going to be a blast playing that song live. He imagined every concert starting with that song only to explode into one of their big up-tempo hits, like Back Roads or Nothing Left to Lose.

This is what happens next. How we get from here to there. I could hold a grudge but it would hold me down.

He watched her as the words came through the speakers. She wouldn't recognize this part, but the…

She suddenly turned the radio way down. "You must get tired of hearing that song," she said. "Do you?"

There was something tweaked about her. Something ramped and he tilted his head. "You don't like that song?" he asked.

"No," she said but she was lying. "I love it. I love all your songs. I'm a fan."

"But not that one. You don't have to lie. You're allowed not to like a song."

"It's just so intense."

"Have you listened to the new album?"

She nodded. "Some of it."

Well, that explained how she hadn't recognized the words. It was criminal of him to feel relief.

Tell her. Tell her right now.

She turned the radio back on just as This is Forgiveness faded out and the DJ launched into an old Taylor Swift song.

She sat back and he boosted the volume to something a little more appropriate.

You are such a coward.

"Do you even have hearing anymore?" she yelled over the chorus.

"What?" he yelled back.

"Exactly."

She'd taken a shower at the hotel and pulled her long blond hair up on top of her head where it was in a tight damp knot. He wanted to put his finger into the center of it. He wanted to pull it loose.

He wanted to ask her more questions about her fiance. He wanted to know who she was smiling at in the picture with the yellow sweater. He wanted to know everything.

He turned down the music once Taylor was done and it had moved on to one of the new groups that didn't sound like music at all. Just electronic distortion and auto-tune.

"You don't like that song?" she asked.

"It's not a song," he said.

"You must be excited that your album is doing so well," she said.

"Yeah," he nodded, but he didn't want to talk about that album. He was a coward through and through.

She wasn't wearing any makeup. And it had been a while since he'd seen a woman without makeup. That was strange, wasn't it? He didn't live with a woman. So he didn't get to have those unguarded fully human moments that came with cohabitation.

Jo always came to work in her war paint, as she called it. And every other woman who came into contact with him or the band was dressed to impress. The whole nine.

Helen was beautiful without makeup.

"Your daughter?" he said changing the subject. "What's her name?"

"Bea. Short for Beatrice."

"How old is she?"

"Three. Like, totally three. She is fully and completely three."

"It's all violence and love," Micah said.

"You should write that down," she said. "All violence and love. That's a good line."

He wrote it down, watching her smile as he did it.

"You spend a lot of time with three-year-olds?"

"My brother is seven years younger than me. I did a lot of babysitting."

"It sounds like you still are."

Well, that was a direct hit. He turned to look out the window, trying to get his bearings. She kept taking his feet out from under him.

"Sorry," she said. "I don't really know you enough to say that kind of thing."

"You know more than most," he said. Their eyes caught when she glanced over and they were right back in that hallway. All that heat between them.

He took a tremendous risk and touched her. He touched her because she needed it and he wanted it. He cupped the back of her neck with his hand.

"I can't…" She stopped. Licked her lips. Her breath was short and gaspy, and he wondered what it would take to convince her to pull over to the side of the road and let him get his hands up her skirt.

"What?"

"I can't really think when you touch me," she breathed, and he took his hand away from her skin.

She was gripping the steering wheel so hard her knuckles were white.

"Is this, like, a joke? Or something?" she asked.

"Is what a joke?"

"Like pretending to be interested in me, or whatever." She shrugged like it was no big deal but she was lying.

"I'm not pretending anything," he said. He couldn't pretend *this*.

"Because if it's a trick, and you're like trying to see how far the sad, lonely widow is going to go—"

"Helen. Pull over."

"I'm just saying it's not a funny trick."

"Pull the fucking car over," he said.

She took one look at his face, quickly hit the signal and pulled over to the side of the road, the wheels bouncing off asphalt onto gravel.

She put the car in Park and then rested her hands in her lap, her eyes out the windshield.

"It's just…" she started in a whisper.

"What?"

"So strange that someone like you would be interested in someone like me."

There were about a million things he could say. Two of which were the truth: that he'd been infatuated with her as a teenager and she'd inspired his new album. But both those things would only create more questions.

"Look at me," he said. And she did. Young and fucking gorgeous and nervous and proud. He wanted to take her hand and put it on his dick. *Does this feel like a trick?* he'd ask.

Instead, he cupped her cheeks in his hands, his thumb on the edge of her lips. She was nervous and she licked her lips, her tongue touching his thumb, and he almost fucking lost it right there. Her breath was coming hard and fast, and he could see her nipples beneath the camisole she wore. Hard and ripe and fucking asking for it. All of her was asking for it. And she knew it.

It took all his strength but he moved slow, giving her all the opportunities to back away, to push him off. But she only sat there, quivering.

He kissed her. Soft lips, slightly chapped. She gasped and he could taste the inside of her mouth. His tongue swept in and he tilted her head and she wrapped her fingers in his shirt and they went up in flames. Hot and hard. Nothing and then inferno.

She made this sound in her throat. A moany, needy sound, and he was ready to pull her into his lap and give her everything he had, just to hear that sound again.

All at once, she leaned back, breaking the kiss and he let her go. They were breathing hard and he wiped a hand over his mouth, wet from her mouth.

"I…ah…um."

"I'm not fucking joking, Helen," he said.

She was silent for a long time and when he looked over at her she was staring right at him. "Why?"

He reached out, ran a hand all along her neck and felt the goose bumps and the breaking of her breath, the pounding of her heart. And then he grabbed her hand and put it on his chest, where his own heart pounded. This was the moment for him to tell the truth. Because she'd made an impact on him when they were young. Because she was imprinted somewhere on his soul.

But he went with a more basic truth.

"Because I feel it, too."

After a moment she pulled against his hand and he let her go. "We should…"

"Sure," he said.

She started up the truck and pulled back onto the empty highway. The silence wasn't awkward, it was only loaded. Heavy. Each of them caught up in their own thoughts about the other.

The navigation told her to take the next exit and they were only a few minutes from their destination.

"Hey, what are we doing here?" she asked. "At your bass player's house? Are we picking him up and taking him with us?"

She looked over at him and then back at the road and then back at him when he stayed silent.

"Micah?"

Shit. He'd forgotten to tell her.

"We're firing him."

CHAPTER
Fourteen

Helen

You have arrived at your destination, the voice on her phone chirped.

"Is this…are you sure?" she asked. Because from what she could tell, the destination was a dirt road leading nowhere.

"Yeah. His cabin is just on the other side of the hill. That's the driveway."

She did not turn down that driveway.

"Helen."

"Why are you firing him?"

"Because the band voted," he said.

"Why do they want him out?"

"Because he's…he's not a stage performer. He's amazing in the studio and a brilliant song writer, but he's not the guy you need in front of thousands of people."

"Can he learn to be?"

"Probably. But we need someone who can pull their weight right now. The band is not wrong. The band is not ever wrong, really."

"Still, you don't want to do this, do you?"

"No," he said. "I don't." He gave her his little lopsided grin that made him look like a kid who'd tracked in the mud, and he was real sorry about that. Over the course of this drive she'd been creating a catalog of Micah Sullivan facial expressions.

There was the *I'm charming and I know it.*

There was the *Please don't recognize me.* They got that one when they stopped for gas and more coffee.

There was the *I'm listening to everything you say and memorizing it for some purpose you will never know about.* He'd looked at her like that the whole time she'd been talking about Evan. God. Evan. It was so strange talking about him...to Micah Sullivan, of all people.

And her current favourite—*I am going to fuck you until you see stars.*

Yeah. That was a real good one.

It had been difficult to believe it, honestly. But the kiss helped. Hoo-boy, that kiss... She hadn't been kissed like that, maybe ever. No offense to Evan, but he didn't kiss her like he was going to die without her. Like he *needed* her. It was the kind of kiss that changed what you thought was possible. Her body was still lit up from it and would be for days. Weeks, probably.

Years.

She turned down the driveway, bumping over the ruts. The meadows on either side of the truck were full of grass and mustard plants and lilacs in bloom. Spring in New York State was a really pretty thing. At the top of the hill, a small cabin and a body of water that wasn't quite a lake but was bigger than a pond were visible.

It was beautiful. Removed and rustic. Totally still. The sun was setting behind them and turning the pond gold.

"The bass player for your band lives here?"

"No. A bass player I have to fire lives here."

A door opened and a man stepped out onto the covered porch. He wore a blue sweater and had long dark hair. He lifted his hand and smiled as she pulled to a stop in the gravel driveway.

"Are you sure you have to do this?"

"Sadly, yes."

"I'll wait here," she said, turning off the car.

"I can't just fire him and leave," he said. "I have to warm up to the conversation."

She groaned.

"I won't have the conversation in front of you," Micah said. "I'll take him for a walk. I promise."

Danny smiled at them from the porch, beckoning them inside. "God, he seems so nice."

"He is. That's the problem. He's too nice for Band of Outlaws." He popped open his door and stepped out of the truck. "Danny!" he yelled.

"Micah. I'm happy to see you."

"You too, brother," Micah said, and the two men hugged.

Helen climbed out of the car feeling like she was going to be watching an execution.

Inside, the cabin was…well, both amazing and a mess, and Helen didn't do a very good job of reacting to the whole of it. She stared, mouth open, at the floor-to-ceiling windows, the musical instruments on top of musical instruments. Recording equipment —mics and amps and speakers and miles of cords wrapped round everything. There was a kitchen, or at least a fridge and a sink that looked like it had a plant growing in it. And over everything, like a layer of dust, were books.

Piles and piles of books.

"Come in, come in," Danny said. "Let me…just…" He took an accordion out of what looked like a very comfortable chair and set it on the floor. He pulled one of those Irish drums off another. "Would you like a drink?" he asked. "I can offer you water, coffee or my new batch of sake."

"Sake?" she said, only because it was a word that did not belong.

"Oh, perfect!" Danny clapped his hands and ran over to the plant sink to pull some cups down from a cupboard. "This batch is best cold," he said, taking a bottle from the fridge. "And I'm glad you're doing to try it. I think it's quite good. But once you have a second glass, just about anything is good."

He came over with a tiny porcelain cup and handed it to Helen. He poured a glass of water from the sink and handed it to Micah and then poured himself a tiny glass of sake. They did a quick cheers standing in the entryway and suddenly, without really understanding how this had all happened, Helen was doing a shot of sake.

"What do you think?" Danny asked.

"It burns," she wheezed.

"But in a good way, right?"

"I guess?"

He took their glasses back to the sink. "You didn't have any sake," she said to Micah.

"I don't drink," he said.

She blinked. Band of Outlaws had their share of drinking songs and she had to admit that drinking seemed kind of part of the culture. "But you and your brother went out for beers. Before the fight."

"He drinks them," he said. "I quit drinking after that fight at The Grammy's. Addiction runs in my family and I knew I couldn't handle it anymore after that fight."

He turned to face her fully and she mirrored him, feeling braced someplace deep and low for a body blow. "I'm going to say a name," he said. "See if you remember it."

"Okay."

"Emmaline Bassiter. She went by the name Emmy. Emmy Bassiter."

"How…how am I supposed to know her?"

"She had long brown hair. Like to her butt. And she sang. A lot. She had a real good voice."

"Is she another singer?" she asked, totally confused.

"Okay!" Danny said, coming up with another round. "One more drink and then you'll stay for dinner? I'm making risotto tonight. I found beautiful chicken-of-the-woods mushrooms in the forest yesterday. Really. It's going to be very good." He handed everyone a glass and Helen tried not to take it. "Please," he said with an exceedingly charming and boyish smile. "I need to make an announcement that is best with a drink."

"Okay," she said and took the drink.

"Kanpai!" Danny said, and they all downed their drinks. More burning. Her eyes watered.

"Before you say anything, Danny," Micah stepped in. "I'm so sorry for what my brother said. He's a dick, he really is."

"I will not argue with you about your brother being a dick. He's not a guy I want to play music with, but he only said what needed to be said. I quit, Micah. I'm sorry, but I quit."

HELEN WENT OUTSIDE DOWN by the pond to give them the privacy to talk. Her head swam from the sake on an empty stomach.

Emmaline Bassiter. That was a really memorable name, but it didn't ring any bells. And what did she have to do with his not drinking?

Her phone in her back pocket buzzed and she pulled it out, surprised to see a text from Jonah. He wasn't much of a texter.

Did you find out how he heard of us?

Gosh, he really was a dog with a bone. *Not yet. I'll find out.*

And then it hit her. The connection between how Micah heard of Haven House might be Emmaline Bassiter.

Do you remember a woman named Emmaline Bassiter?

No, should I?

I think she might have gone to Haven House.

You want me to have Elise look into it?

Yeah.

Why wouldn't he just tell her? she wondered. Was he ashamed of this Emmaline woman? Was that why he wanted his donation to be anonymous?

"Helen!" She turned to see Micah standing at the back door. "It's safe to come back up."

She walked back through the golden sunshine to the modest cabin full of music and instruments. "You okay?" she asked, Micah as she walked by him.

"I'm sad," he said. "But I'll get over it."

"How is Danny?" she asked.

"Relieved. You know, it's been so long since someone didn't want what I have that I'd forgotten there were so many ways to be successful in music. He likes his life. Far be it from me to fuck it up for him."

She put her hand on his shoulder, his chest, really. Right over his heart, the same place he'd put her hand in the car. He lifted her fingers and pressed his lips to them and she sucked in a breath. It happened so fast the way he turned her on. Like she was herself standing there and in the next minute she was starved for him. So on fire she didn't even recognize herself.

His eyes caught hers and for a second she tried to hide it. Tried to look away and make a joke, but he looked at her not just like he knew what she was feeling. But that he felt it too.

"What is this?" she whispered.

"Chemistry," he said.

Is that all? she thought, and pulled her hand away.

"Are we staying for dinner?" she asked.

"It's up to you. Danny would love it and the guy can seriously cook."

"I'm starving."

"Me too."

"So, I guess we're staying for dinner."

"Go on inside," he said. "I'm going to make a fire."

She went inside, only because she needed a second to get her bearings. To put herself together. *Chemistry,* he says, like it's nothing.

And that was the thing. He might feel the same way she did,

but it didn't have the same effect on his life as it did on hers. Perspective, she thought.

She pulled open the screen door, stepped inside and immediately kicked over a tuba. "Oh my gosh, I'm sorry." She scrambled to pick it up and knocked over some sheet music stacked on a speaker.

"Don't worry," Danny said, standing in the kitchen, stirring a pot on the stove. Whatever he was making had transformed the smell of the place until it was nothing but garlic and butter. She could lick the walls. "I need to clean out this stuff, but I don't."

She laughed at his self-acceptance.

"Where did you get all of this?" Helen asked, standing up and picking her way across the room toward the kitchen.

"Well, I inherited most of it from my dad. He was a piano tuner at Eastman College." Danny looked around at all his stuff like they were treasures. "He thought he could fix everything. And usually he could. The tuba might be a lost cause, though."

He was grating cheese over the risotto and then chucking in handfuls of chopped parsley.

"Try it?" he asked, holding out the wooden spoon. She took a nibble of the risotto and it was—as advertised—delicious.

"Perfect," she said. He beamed at her and started to go through a drawer, pulling out chipped china and spoons. "How did you and Micah meet?" she asked, taking a tarnished silver spoon he handed her.

"Online," he said, and started spooning risotto into the bowls. "I'd duet with his TikToks, but like, with an accordion," he said, pointing over her shoulder. "Or a slide whistle. Once a pan flute I've got around here. And he just contacted me."

"That must have been something." Micah Sullivan contacting a guy out of the blue.

"Nah," he said. "People contact me all the time."

Yeah, she could see why Micah liked this guy. He was completely unfazed by Micah's fame. "We started working together in the evenings. Writing songs. Working out arrangements. When it came time to work out the album he came here. It was fun."

"And then he asked you to be in the band?"

"Not fun," he said seriously. "But I figured I should try, you know. Just to see if being in one of the world's biggest rock and roll bands was better than it seemed like it would be."

"And it wasn't?"

He leaned against the counter like they were old friends talking about another old friend and not the biggest rock band in the world.

"They weren't together very long before that first song of theirs blew up, and now they're kind of forced together whether they like it or not. Like an arranged marriage."

She laughed. She laughed so hard she hooted just as Micah came in from the back door. He'd pulled a red stocking cap over his hair and it made him look like a very sexy rock and roll lumberjack.

"What are you guys laughing about?" he asked, and she got the impression that he loved that they were getting along so well. It was a nice feeling when people you liked liked each other, proving your taste in people was good.

"Danny just said Band of Outlaws was like an arranged marriage," she said. "Because that song was such a hit so fast and now you have to be together."

"For the sake of the kids," Danny said.

"To keep up appearances."

"Did you guys drink more sake?" Micah asked, like he was confused.

"No!" Danny said. "But that is an excellent idea."

"You want me to take out some guitars?" Micah asked.

"Another excellent idea!" Danny said, they were like two boys building a ramp for their bikes. "Can you play the harmonica?" Danny was looking at Helen when he asked that question.

"Me? No."

"Tambourine?"

"Probably not."

"How about that tuba?" Micah asked.

He was joking with her. There was a lightness to him that made him almost unrecognizable. Like, he was always flirting, but there was an old-hand feel to it. This was strangely joyful, as if they were inside a million little jokes.

She hadn't felt this way outside of her family in three long years.

"The tuba doesn't work," Danny said.

"That's too bad," she said. "I'm very good on a tuba."

"Really?" Danny asked, all hope.

"She's kidding," Micah sighed dramatically and took two acoustic guitars out to the fire.

"Here," Danny said and started loading Helen up with dishes and forks. "I've never seen him like this," he murmured.

"Like what?"

"This happy. He's like a kid. He never acts like a kid."

She felt herself blushing and wanting to believe something that could not be true. That he was happy because of her. It just didn't make sense. Before lockdown he'd been dating supermodels. And it wasn't just about beauty—she wasn't some kind of nightmare to look at—it was about a big, glamorous life.

And she had nothing to offer in that world.

"I'm glad he finally worked up the nerve to call you," he said.

"What?" she asked. "Worked up what nerve?"

Danny blinked at her, a dollop of risotto slipping from the spoon into the bowl. And he looked very very guilty. "Please forget I said that."

Micah opened the screen door and pushed his head in, bringing with him the smell of smoke and lake. "Come on. These instruments aren't going to play themselves."

"And this risotto isn't going to eat itself," Danny said. Helen had no choice but to follow them out to the firepit.

What Danny had said felt like something she needed to get to the bottom of, but the fire was spectacular against the indigo night. The air was just that right amount of cool. And the risotto was warm and smelled delicious.

And it didn't really seem to matter right then.

There were three Adirondack chairs and she took the one that didn't have a guitar resting in it. Micah and Danny wolfed down their food like teenage boys and put down their bowls so they could pick up their guitars.

She ate with a bit more decorum, and whatever she'd expected when they started to play, it didn't come close to the reality. They sang songs by the Beatles and Van Morrison. Danny had a fabulous take on a Prince song. He rearranged a Shawn Mendes tune so it was punk rock.

"Okay," Micah said. "Try and guess this one." He started to play a song that sounded like classical music and looked at both of them. "Nothing?"

She was never going to be good at this game, but then a note hit her and she laughed. "It's that Billie Eilish song."

"Give the girl a prize," he said.

It was a beautiful night. A beautiful fire and the music...she was never going to do this justice when she told Jonah about it. It felt like she was getting something so special, so rare. Not just the music, but this version of Micah. She thought of all those magazine articles and the slick photo spreads. Him and his brother, looking stern and rock and roll. She'd known he was charming in an awe-shucks kind of way; she'd seen the interviews on Ellen and Jimmy Fallon.

But he was smart. And he was engaged. And just like the fire in front of them, he sent out sparks. That must have been what made him a rock star—the sparks.

She took her phone out of her pocket and Micah stopped playing, the guitar notes cut off with a jangle.

"What are you doing?" he asked, and it dawned on her that he thought she was recording this.

"I'm just...I'm texting my mom. Letting her know I won't be home tonight. I swear, I'm not...I wouldn't."

"Yeah," he said and looked chagrined. "I'm sorry. Just…habit."
It occurred to her that this was rare for him, too. And that made it
even more special.

I won't be home tonight, she wrote. And then put her phone in
her pocket and settled back against the chair.

There was a pinch in her chest thinking about Bea; Helen
hadn't spent a night away from her since she was born. But there
was enough consistent love on that farm to light up a small city,
and in the morning she'd call and talk to her.

Her stomach full, her heart happy, she let the once-in-a-life-
time moment wash over her.

"Let's play something from the new album," Danny said.

Micah's head came up quick, like he didn't like the idea. Like
Danny had said something he shouldn't have.

"I've got a better idea," Micah said and fished a napkin out of
his pocket. "I've got something new."

"Yeah?"

"Chorus and bridge. Follow me?"

*This is what you deserve and you know it. This is what you should
have and you want it. I'm relentless for you and you like it.*

It was that thing she'd said at the diner. He was making a song
out of something she'd said. And it was sexy. Like, undeniably
sexy. She remembered the grip of his hand on the back of her
neck. The way he'd put his arm on the door frame beside her head
in the hotel hallway.

The beat of his heart against her hand.

"Let's try it in G minor," Danny said. They played it again.
"Move the chorus to the bridge," Danny said.

They sang it again.

"Damn it," Micah said. "That's better."

"I know."

"I'll have to give you co-writing credit on this one, too. You
and Helen."

"I just said the word relentless," Helen said. "That hardly
seems like it deserves a co-writing credit."

"I don't know," Micah said, the fire turning his face gold. "The right word at the right time is the difference between fine and epic."

"Why don't you give Alex any writing credits on your songs?" Danny asked, picking quietly at his guitar. Micah looked up, his face sharp with shadow.

"Because he doesn't write any of them."

"Doesn't that seem strange?"

"I am sorry about what Alex said to you," Micah said, his voice a low murmur through the velvet night, the sparkling fire. "He's a bona fide asshole."

"You apologize for him a lot."

"He's my brother!"

"I'm sorry, you're right," Danny said and picked out a few chords. Micah joined him and then Danny stopped. "Really, though. You should talk to your brother. Like, stop fighting and talk. That's my two cents and all I'm going to say." He went hard into the first chords of the Bleachers song that they did with Springsteen and it was one of Helen's favorites.

Micah wanted to be angry. To nurse whatever darkness his brother called up in him. But the night had been so great and she didn't want to see it spoiled.

When Helen opened her mouth and started to sing, both men looked at her, startled. She didn't have an amazing voice, but it wasn't bad. She'd sung in high school, and if the melody didn't get fancy she could hang.

Micah lit up like she'd opened a million bottles of champagne. Like she'd thrown open the door to a circus and a party. It was heady. Exciting. Affirming.

No one, not even Evan, had looked at her like that. Evan's love had been solid. And steady. He'd looked at her like she was his partner and he was lucky to have her.

This look, from Micah, was something altogether different.

CHAPTER
Sixteen

MICAH

She fell asleep. In the splintering Adirondack chair, she was all curled up and snoring just a little. Just enough to be audible over the crackle of the dying fire.

"You called her," Danny said.

"I did."

"Does she know?"

"What?" He'd given her his mother's name, she would connect those dots soon enough. He was tired of pretending and it was going to come out sooner or later.

"About…the album. The songs?"

"No."

"You should tell her."

Tell her that he wrote an album about her. About her life. About the death of her fiancé. *Yeah*, something told him, *she wouldn't see it as a compliment.* She wouldn't fan girl, she'd feel violated. And he couldn't blame her. Because he'd mined her tragedy for his own gain.

No. She wouldn't fan girl. And it was only one of the things he liked about her.

"My brother said the same thing," Micah said.

"We agree on that, at least."

"He thinks I should pay her."

"I don't agree with that."

Yeah, Micah didn't either. It made it cheap somehow, when what she'd brought into his life was priceless.

"We should get on the road," he said, glancing at his phone. It was midnight, which was usually the beginning of his night. The hour he was coming alive, and she was all curled up in that chair, her denim coat too thin to protect against the chill in the night.

"The bunkie is all set up," Danny said. "If you want to stay."

"You evicted the mice?"

"Relocated. And there are clean sleeping bags and pillows out there."

"I'll see what she wants," Micah said. Danny stood up and grabbed the guitars. Left the dishes stacked by the fire. He went inside, the door squeaking and then clicking shut.

"What do you want?" he whispered, looking at her face, thinking impossible thoughts. Wishing what she wanted was him. He crouched in front of her. "Helen?"

She woke like no one else he knew. Asleep one second and then fully awake in the next. It was startling.

"Is everything okay?" she asked, slipping her feet down onto the ground like she was ready to run.

"Fine." He smiled at her. "You fell asleep."

"What time is it?"

"Midnight. You want to get on the road?"

"I told my parents I wouldn't be home tonight." She yawned wide.

"We can stay here. Danny has a bunkie."

"What's a bunkie?"

He gave into the temptation to stroke some of the hair off her face. Sleepy, she was younger than she seemed when she was fully awake and being bossy. "Come on," he said. He took her hand and pulled her out of the chair.

But he pulled too hard, and she was light, and she bumped into his body. Again, without flinching. And he felt her from his shoulders to his knees and through all of his bones.

"Show me this bunkie," she whispered, her eyes luminous in the night.

The teenage boy he hadn't been for a very long time wondered what might happen in the bunkie. A kiss seemed like a sure thing and an impossibility at the same time.

"You guys sounded so good tonight," she said. Her shoulder pressed against his. Her wrist brushed his.

"Yeah, Danny brings out the best in other musicians. He's like a supercharged battery or something."

"That's why you wanted him to be a part of the band?"

"And I like him."

"Do you like the rest of the band?"

"Don't listen to Danny. He thinks everything should be as simple as music. And a band is far from simple."

Her eyes were on him and he took her elbow to walk her around a rock so she didn't trip. "That doesn't make sense."

"It's because you've never been in a band."

He pushed open the door to the bunkie, which was basically a little shed on the edge of the lake. But it had a queen-size bed, beautiful views of the sunrise and a sink that was usually used to clean fish. Once the quarantine lifted, he'd spent a few months in this bunkie, writing music and arranging it with Danny. Fishing and hiking and eating the good food Danny made. It had been the best kind of summer camp.

"You can sleep here," he said.

"Where are you going to sleep?"

"I'll take the tuba off the chair in the cabin."

"No," she said and reached for his hand. "That's ridiculous. Sleep here."

"There's only one bed, Helen."

"I'm aware, Micah. If I promise to keep my hands to myself—"

Something snapped in him, the thin tether he'd had on his self-control since the closet. He stepped up very close to her. Crowding her, thinking she would step back.

But she didn't.

"I don't want to make that promise," he whispered. He could feel the rise and fall of her stomach against his. Fuck, he wanted to pull off their clothes, feel that skin against his. It would be soft. He was sure of it. The softest thing he'd ever touched.

"I don't either." She grabbed him, hands full of his shirt right at his ribs, holding him in place. Her eyes locked on his chin. And she was into it, he could tell, but something was bothering her.

"What are you thinking?"

"This isn't a thing I do," she finally said. "And maybe this isn't all that different for you?"

"It's different."

"I just don't know…how to be cool."

"You're plenty cool."

She narrowed her eyes. "Don't patronize me just to try and get in my pants."

"I would never. I think you're one of the most authentic people I've ever met and that makes you very cool."

"Micah—"

"I think you're cool. And beautiful. And sexy and real…so fucking real you blow the top of my head off."

He watched a whole avalanche of emotions chase themselves across her face. "I want to kiss you," she said.

"I'm agreeable to this."

"I'm just…it's been a while."

"We kissed, like, a few hours ago. And trust me, you did just fine."

"No, the rest of it. The after kissing part." She blew out a long breath. "It's been so long, Micah."

He stroked back her hair with the flat of his hand, and her

head tilted back on her neck, like he had total control of her. He liked that. He liked that a lot. "You think you've forgotten how?"

"Maybe," she laughed.

"Would it make you feel better if I told you it had been a while for me, too?"

"No. Because I wouldn't believe you."

He shrugged. "It was a long lockdown. And before that, I wasn't hooking up as much as the tabloids would have you think."

"But before that?" she asked.

"What do you want to hear?" He stiffened, surprised she was even going there. Lots of women got off on his stories; they liked the idea of trying to one-up some nameless, faceless woman.

He just hadn't thought she would be one of them.

"That you know what you're doing."

He laughed. God, she was a surprise. Softly, he kissed her lips. And then harder. Until her arms were around his neck and her mouth was open against his.

"You worried I won't get you off?" he asked, and she sucked in a breath at his words. He filed that away. She liked words.

"No. I mean…maybe? Not because of you. But because of me?"

"You want to come?" he asked.

She pulled a breath in through her nose so deeply her nostrils flared. And then nodded.

"Say it, Helen."

"You say it."

"I'm going to make you come."

She moaned, her eyes all but rolling back in her head. "Micah," she breathed. "Please."

Yeah, he was a goner for her.

Her body melted into his and it felt like a victory. Like something he'd earned and he savored it. Her belly against his. Her breasts. The tops of her thighs. The lock of her arms behind his back.

He put his hands in her hair, pulling loose that bun so it all fell down around her shoulders, across his arms. It was still damp in places from being washed earlier, and he didn't know why but he liked that. How intimate it was.

Against her belly, he was hard and she pressed into him. Behind his eyelids he saw sparks. Stars. Fuck.

Gasping for air, he pulled away from the kiss, pressed his lips to her neck, the soft skin under her jaw. She tilted back her head, letting him go where he wanted. His pulled her earlobe into his mouth, raked his teeth across it and she shook.

Oh, fuck, this kind of honesty was going to kill him. Literally end him.

He kissed his way down her neck and along the edge of the camisole that had been making him crazy. The freckles he couldn't see in the moonlight, but that he'd spent the day memorizing.

There was one here. Right above her collarbone. Another here, near the strap of the camisole. Another one there, at the rise of her breast. He opened his lips, breathing her in. Licking her skin.

He went further. Bent deeper. Took more. His hand cupped her breast and she gasped, pulling him up to kiss.

Oh, she kissed him like there were secrets she needed to know buried inside. He kissed her back the same way. Sanity slipping. He pushed aside the camisole and touched her bare skin. Her breast, warm and full, was in his hand. The nipple hard under his fingers.

He broke the kiss, bent to pull her nipple into his mouth. Hard. Fierce. She rose up on her tiptoes, crying out.

"Helen?"

"More, please, oh my god, just…more."

Suddenly nothing was slow and nothing was careful. It was need. It was years of it. She was the girl who'd sat with him at his lowest time so he wouldn't be alone and he was wild to thank her. To show her what it meant to him.

She was the woman in the article, baring her soul and doing

the impossible, and he wanted to show her what that meant to him.

He tore her shirt off and he could not get enough of her skin. He wanted to feel all of her with all of him.

He lifted her up and she wrapped her legs around his waist and her arms around his neck, clutching his head to her chest. His kissed his way from breast to breast, pulling her nipples into his mouth. Sucking her until her skin was damp. He took the three steps from the door to the bed, aware of how hot she was between her legs, pressed up against him. How wet. He bumped into the bed and laid her down, she didn't let go of him and he was pulled down on top of her.

They fit together perfectly.

Her fingers made their way up under his shirt, across his stomach. Her thumb brushed his nipple, and he hissed and groaned.

"Take it off," she whispered, and the words weren't totally out of her mouth before both his shirts were off. The necklaces around his neck fell against her skin, without his shirt in the way. She laid her hand against them, pressing them against the warmth of her body, and it was strange and lovely.

"What are they?" she asked. "The necklaces."

"You want to talk about that now?"

"I might forget later."

He kissed her fingers, moving them out of his way. "St. Christopher from my mom when I dropped out of high school and started playing music on the road. And..." He lifted the second one, the squiggle of metal. "I have no idea where this came from or why I wear it."

"You're kidding."

"I think a stylist on a magazine shoot gave it to me and I just liked it. You were expecting more?"

"I don't know what to expect with you," she said. "You're constantly surprising."

She grabbed his face and pulled it to hers. Kissing him without any restraint or finesse. Just joy and need. Like they were discovering sex for the first time all over again. God, how long since he'd felt this way?

He kissed her shoulder. The tender bend of her elbow. He kissed the part of her waist where it tucked in just before flaring out over her hipbone. Her skirt had been pulled down a little, and he kissed the rise of flesh just under her belly button.

He grabbed her hand, kissed the knobby bone of that tantalizing wrist. The center of her palm. He licked her longest finger and pulled it into his mouth.

Her eyes flared and she arched against the bed. "You're killing me, Micah."

He pulled her fingers free of his mouth and bent to her breasts again. His beard was growing in and he knew that she was going to have beard rash on her skin in the morning, and he liked that idea. Liked it so much he pulled at the soft skin at the top of her breast into his mouth, hard enough to leave a mark.

"What are you doing?" She laughed. "We're not teenagers."

"You get a lot of hickeys when you were a teenager?" he asked, feeling like a teenager.

"What's a lot?" she asked.

"More than one."

"Then yes."

He growled and got up on his knees over her hips and began kissing her breasts in earnest. Sloppy, sucking kisses that make her squeal and shriek and laugh, and he loved it so much he didn't stop until she clapped a hand over his mouth. "Stop it," she said. And he nodded.

She sighed, her hands back up in his hair. More kissing.

Kissing and kissing. Until all the laughter stopped and it was just the two of them, skin to skin. He made his way down her belly to the waist of that skirt.

"Micah," she breathed.

"Do you want me to stop?"

"No. God, no."

He eased off the bed until he was on his knees between her spread legs. From this angle she was so…perfect. Like she was a queen. He hated that this angle was somehow reserved for porn. There should be way more art of women like this. Arms thrown over their heads, backs arched in pleasure. Skin flushed. Nipples red and dampened. Total feminine surrender and power.

A guitar lick ran through his head.

Fuck, he thought. That's a first. A song idea while about to go down on a woman.

This woman. This goddamn woman…

Another guitar lick. He almost laughed with the sheer delight of it.

He pushed her skirt, which was twisted around her thighs, up to her waist. She wore black cotton underwear. And he realized they were the ones he'd bought this morning and fucking loved that. Some fierce Neanderthal in him wanted her to only wear the things he'd bought online for her, guessing at her size and worried about being presumptuous.

She spread her legs wider, giving him all the room he needed, then lifted up her hips, begging him to come closer. And so he put his mouth against her, over the cotton. She was damp and salty, soaking through the fabric. She moaned.

Yeah, he liked it, too.

Pushing the cotton aside, he came face-to-face with the pink of her. The sweet, delicious tang of her. She lifted her foot, planting it on the bed, and he slipped his arms around her hips, hauling her down the mattress closer to him. Closer to his mouth.

And then he kissed her. Licked her. Slipped his tongue between the fat pink folds. Found all of her; mapped a trail from her clit to the sweet entrance of her body. Found those places that made her shake and then worked them until they made her moan. Until she was holding his head against her, grinding herself into him. Crying out his name.

He slipped fingers inside of her. As many as she could take until he found that spot. The let's-go spot. And her legs curled up and her body bowed back and the sound that came out of her was the sweetest sound he'd ever heard.

And then, in one long slow exhale, she reversed it. Her legs flopped wide like she had no bones. Her hands stroked his hair and then drifted to his shoulders. The keening cry of her orgasm shifted into a happy, contended sigh that also delighted him. He sat back, caught her eye and wiped his mouth, slick with her come.

"Josie said you'd be good at this," she laughed.

CHAPTER
Seventeen

Helen

Immediately she knew it had been the wrong thing to say.

I mean…so stupid. So totally stupid. And she clung to the idea that maybe he hadn't heard her. Or that other women had said far more stupid things after he'd given them the kind of orgasm that didn't happen every damn day and her stupid thing would be no big deal.

But he'd heard her.

And whatever stupid things other people had said, what she'd said hurt him.

He sat back on his heels, his face turned away. High color on his cheekbones.

"Micah," she breathed and sat up. God, she was so wet and the pressure on her clit sent sparks through her body. She didn't want it to end like this. She didn't want it to end at all. "That was…I'm sorry."

He braced his hands against the bed, his fingers inches from her legs, but she could feel them. The heat of them. The exact and precise distance between his fingers and her legs.

Those fingers that had been inside of her. That if she grabbed and held to her face would smell like her. If she put them in her mouth, they'd taste like her, and she'd blown it and he would never touch her again.

And worse, she'd never get to touch him.

"Josie is my cousin and I told her about that moment in the hotel, outside my door. About how it had seemed like you were going to kiss me…"

He smiled at her, but not his good smile. Not the smile from around the fire. This was the smile he gave the people at the county jail. The *yeah, yeah, sure* smile.

Parts of her heart snapped off.

She didn't know how to get from this smile to the one she wanted.

"She said I should just go for it," she whispered.

"And you did," he said. "You want a selfie?"

She gasped.

"Sorry," he said and shrugged into his shirt.

"No. I'm…I'm so sorry. You just…that was about me. That comment. Not about you."

He looked at her, his hair pushed back from his face. His rock-and-roll armor in place. And she wanted to say *I'm just a normal person, and I don't know how to do this with another normal person, much less my favorite singer.*

But when his eyes met hers, she realized he knew all that. And what was at the heart of all of this was that he was a normal person, too. She'd just forgotten that.

"Yeah," he said. "It's like I said in the closet. It's never really about me."

CHAPTER
Eighteen

MICAH

Yeah, he thought, filling a bucket of water at the sink to take outside and throw across the embers of the fire. Maybe he could have handled that better. It wasn't the first time he'd heard something like that after sex. It wasn't even the hundredth.

He knew in excruciating detail how he couldn't have things both ways. He couldn't be famous and one of the sexiest men alive, according to various magazines that claimed some kind of authority over that domain, and he couldn't use that famous sexiness to his advantage when it came down to making money for the band.

And then wish it all away when it suited him.

It couldn't be done.

But this moment—this thing with Helen—felt outside of that. She was kissing him just like he was kissing her—because they were people interested in each other. Attracted to each other. Wanted each other.

But part of wanting him was the persona he'd created. Nothing was outside of Band of Outlaws.

You can't have it both ways.

"Hey." Danny came into the room from his bedroom. He was wearing pajamas. The guy slept in pajamas.

Danny was always too pure for Band of Outlaws.

"You putting out the fire?" he asked with a yawn. "I was about to."

"I got it. Go on to bed."

"Helen?"

"Sound asleep," he said with a smile he did not feel.

"Okay. See you in the morning," Danny said and toddled off to bed. But at the doorway he turned around. "I know it's not any of my business and you're a real private guy when it comes to, like…girl stuff."

"Girl stuff? Are we in high school?"

"I like her. Helen. I like the way you look at her."

"How do you think I look at her?"

"Like she's real." Danny yawned again. "You don't look at everyone that way."

"I have no idea what you're talking about, man," Micah lied with a laugh, but Danny didn't buy it.

"Yeah, you do," he said, as serious as he'd ever been. And then he lifted his hand in goodbye and vanished into his bedroom.

Micah took the bucket of water, grabbed a blanket from the back of the tuba chair and went back out to the fire. He'd put it out, in a bit. But first he wrapped that blanket around his shoulders and sat back in his chair, watching the orange-blue flames eat up the last of the wood.

I look at everyone like they're real, he thought. *I look at fans like they're real. My band like they're real. You don't get to where I am unless you do that.*

The thing I liked was that she looked at me like I was real.

He pulled his phone out of his pocket and texted his brother.

Danny is out.

You fired him? Came the immediate reply.

No. He quit.

You were the only one who thought that would work.

He could hear his brother's voice. He could hear the laughter buried in those words, like it was just all one more chance for Alex to score a point or two off Micah. Like jerking around poor Danny didn't mean anything.

You still with that girl?

His thumbs paused over the screen, unsure of what to say. Unsure, really, of what had happened.

Suddenly, his phone rang. It was Alex.

"Texting is bullshit," Alex said. "You all right?"

"I'm good. Fine. Why?"

"Look, I'm sorry it didn't work out with Danny. I know you like the kid."

This was Alex's thing, so magnanimous when everything was said and done.

"He's a better musician than all of us," Micah said, because he had to say something.

"That doesn't make him right for Band of Outlaws."

Yeah, he thought. That was the truth, right there.

"This is gonna be good, you'll see," Alex said. "The original lineup, out on the road. New music. Good times. Our fans are going to be so fucking happy."

Yeah, he thought, pulling himself from thoughts of Helen. This was what he was supposed to be thinking about, the band. The tour. The fans.

The music.

People needing something to be happy about. A reason to dance and sing all the words to their favorite songs. He loved being that guy. Lived for it. It was a privilege, really. And that he needed his brother to remind him of that was just par for the course with them.

Alex was a simple guy.

Micah didn't have to complicate things, wanting something that was never his to want.

"You're right," he said.

"Of course, I'm right. Micah, man, you take this shit too seriously. It's only rock and roll."

Micah laughed, because he was supposed to. Because it made his brother happy.

"Good night, brother," he said. "I'll see you tomorrow."

"Yeah. You better. I miss you."

"Miss you, too."

He hung up, pushed his phone back into his pocket and looked up at the stars. There were thousands of them out here. Splashed across the sky.

He thought of that guitar lick he'd come up with while he was between Helen's legs.

Alex was right. Music was simple. Sex was simple. He didn't need to go complicating everything with feelings. He'd write a song about her. Another one. And move on. She'd been a weird diversion in his head anyway. Part of the pandemic. Part of missing his mom. Thinking about the past.

Yeah. It was the music. The band. The fans.

Simple.

CHAPTER

Nineteen

Helen

Sleep happened in fits and starts. Mostly she lay on her side, watching the moon's reflection move across the pond, and tried to make sense of the last twenty-four hours.

The guilt she expected did not arrive. She was 29 years old and Evan would want her to have a full and happy life. With all the good sex she could get. He'd been a solid guy that way. But lying in that sleeping bag she did feel a powerful grief. A surprising, biting grief.

The last person who'd touched her was no longer Evan. Was no longer the father of her baby and the man she'd planned to marry.

It was Micah Sullivan.

And she'd hurt him.

I need to figure out how to make this right.

She must have fallen asleep at some point because the next thing she knew it was daylight and the sky was pink and yellow and full of birds.

The view from the bunkie was, without a doubt, one of the best she'd ever seen.

Her phone in the pocket of her coat buzzed against the hard wood floor. Carefully, so she didn't let in any cool air, she reached out and grabbed it. Ultimately letting in tons of cool air.

The text was from Jonah.

Emmy Bassiter, short for Emmeline, was one of the first Moms we had at Haven House. She stayed for a week.

She pulled in a big breath and let it out. *And the kids?* She texted back.

Only one. A boy. Michael. Age twelve.

Michael.

Micah.

Damn it.

He'd been a Haven House kid.

CHAPTER

Twenty

MICAH

He woke up damp with dew. The sun a pale yellow in a pink and gold sky. So many fucking birds.

"Shit," he muttered and tried to straighten his neck. The fire he'd been planning on putting out was still smoking. The blanket he'd had over his shoulders had been supplemented by a sleeping bag across his legs.

It was all damp, too.

"Good morning."

He turned to see Helen sitting in the other chair. Bathed in the pale yellow and pink and blue of dawn. She smiled at him and he cleared his throat and looked away.

"What time is it?" he asked.

"Six-thirty,' she said. "How's your neck?"

"Fine."

"Liar. Here." A cup of coffee in a travel mug was put in front of him. "Milk no sugar. The way you had it in the diner."

"Thanks," he said trying not to be touched that she'd noticed.

Of course she'd noticed, a dark miserable voice in his head

said. She likes your music, she likes your band, she probably made note of everything you said and did.

Even as he thought it, he didn't think it was true. And even if it was true, he didn't really care.

He'd noticed the way she drank her coffee. Did that make him an asshole?

She said something in an unguarded moment. Stop trying to turn her into an asshole.

He reached a hand out into the cool air to take the coffee. His fingers were chilled and they burned against the warmth of the mug. "Thank you. That was nice of you."

"You didn't have to sleep out here." Her eyes met his and the night was right there between them. "Just to avoid me."

"I wasn't avoiding you," he said and took a sip. "That's good coffee."

"Danny gave me the history of every bean."

"Sounds like Danny." He shifted in the chair, pushing the blanket off his shoulders. "We should get on the road."

"Is your real name Michael?"

Ah. She knew.

"Yep."

"Your mom—Emmaline. She was in the first group of women at Haven House."

He'd been waiting for this penny to drop. Had, in fact, forced the issue last night, giving her his mom's name, but he still felt that internal flinch.

"Yeah," was all he said.

"Where did the Sullivan come from?"

"My stepdad. Alex's dad. After Haven House, Mom got cleaned up and they got married. He adopted me."

"And Micah?"

"Mom's pet name for me when I was a kid."

She took a sip from her coffee, the steam rising up around her face. Her hair was back up in that bun and he was sucker punched with the memory of it down around her shoulders. How the ends curled over her breasts. Her nipples hidden and revealed.

He sighed and glanced away.

"Why didn't you say something?"

He rolled his neck. "Because part of me wanted you and Jonah to recognize me, and when that didn't happen, I don't know, I felt a little stupid."

"It's not stupid. Nothing about this is stupid. What happened?"

"My mom picked me up from school. Alex would have been about five and we were living in this shitty trailer. Peter had money and a job and a house downtown, but he wouldn't marry Mom unless she stopped drinking and got her shit together. There was a lot of fighting and I think she was scared that Peter would take Alex and so she applied to Haven House. She'd been trying to get clean before we went and I think Haven House might have saved her life."

"Micah," she sighed. "I'm so glad."

"And you might have saved mine." She looked astonished and embarrassed. He ran his fingers through the fringe of the blanket over his shoulders. "They took Mom into this building and your dad tried to distract me with stuff, and I refused to leave the building. I just sat there, waiting for her."

"Wait. I remember that. You...were twelve. I'd been trying to imagine you as a young kid. But you were almost a teenager. I remember this. You sat there like a time bomb and we were so worried you were going to run away."

He did not want it to matter that she remembered him. But something that had been tied up tight in his chest relaxed.

"I'd been about to," he said.

"I sat with you—" She was watching him with those green, green eyes slightly narrowed, like she was working at pulling up the memories.

"You sat with me for hours."

"We had Popsicles and we talked about…music. Micah!" She laughed and he smiled at her.

"Good to see you again, Helen."

"Good to see you too, Michael."

That name shouldn't have meant anything. He hadn't used it for years. It was the name his teachers called on the first day of school and he said "Call me Micah." Michael was the name his stepdad used and just about no one else. But that name in her voice…it was powerful. A punch to the side of his head.

"It's a little foolish to put so much importance on a week we spent in the Catskills," he said, trying to deflect.

"I was ten when my stepdad came into my life," she said. "Everything is really important at that age, especially kindness. And second chances."

Suddenly deeply uncomfortable, he sighed and got to his feet. Revealing this truth between them only highlighted the other secret he was keeping.

The bigger lie he was telling.

"We should get on the road." Get back to his life and the band and the tour.

"I'll take you to White Plains today," she said. "But it would be amazing if we could stop off at Haven House and the Riverview Inn."

"Is this more blackmail?" he asked. "You need me to be in your bachelor sex auction?"

"No." She laughed. "You can say no to this."

He realized that she expected him to say no. In part because of what happened the previous night.

He was being a goddamn teenager.

"I'd love to."

Her smile was a straight-up beam of light, and he blinked and looked over her shoulder at Danny in the kitchen window, watching them with interest.

"And, Micah? Last night—"

"Don't apologize again," he said.

Last night hadn't been about him. It was never going to be about him. He was just happy he could be there for her.

"I won't," she said and then laughed. "Though I am sorry."

"Helen!"

"But also…" She sighed and smiled, her head tilted back to the sun, and he could see on her neck and the top of her chest the beard burn he'd left on her. The faded blue of a hickey.

And that seemed good. Right.

They'd left bruises of all kinds on each other.

"Thank you," she said. "I mean, for real. I thought, maybe, that part of my life was gone. But it was really amazing to feel that way again."

"Orgasmic?"

"Sure," she said. "But also… desired." The flush on her cheeks was burning up her face, leaving blotches on her neck.

And no one could resist her like this, much less him, who had zero experience resisting anything. He stood, the blanket falling to the grass damp with dew, and if she was looking, she'd see his erection.

Helen made a squeaking sound in her throat and he smiled.

Guess she noticed.

He crossed the small circle of the fire pit until he was standing in front of her. She tilted her head back to look at him, her lips parting, her chest rising with a heavy breath. He braced his hands on the arms of her chair and bent down until his face was close to hers. Her lips, which she nervously licked, a breath away.

"It was my pleasure," he whispered.

And then to his total shock, she reached up with chilly fingers and cupped his face holding him still—not that he would move—so she could kiss him.

Shy, at first, for all her boldness, maybe waiting for him to jerk back and away from her. But when he smiled against her lips she opened her mouth and let him in. He pulled her to her feet and then up against his body, his arms wrapped around her waist. He kissed her, and kissed her again, and she put her fingers in his hair and ran her nails down his scalp in a way that gave him shivers. Honest to god, shivers.

From inside the house there was whooping and clapping, and they laughed into each other's mouths. "I think Danny approves," he said.

She leaned back, blinked at him, her lips swollen from their kisses.

Her smile was…radiant.

Radiant and reckless.

Crap. He hung onto that lyric.

Radiant and reckless, I am helpless. Why would I say no to this? When this is all I've ever wanted.

Fuck. That was good. She was really bringing out some seriously good music out of him.

"Micah?" she said, her fingers stroking the wrinkles that popped up between his eyes. "What are you thinking about?"

"You and songs."

She laughed, thinking he was joking. But then she realized he wasn't. "That sounds nice."

"It is," he said with a happy sigh. He threw his arm over her shoulder. "It's real nice."

Helen

He forgave her. That was a relief. As for the rest of it…the kissing? She had no freaking clue.

Maybe it was just a…fling. Just a casual kind of no-strings, rock-star-level fling. They'd stop by the Riverview Inn and Haven House. Alice was going to try and get him to stay for supper, and maybe, just maybe, he could be convinced to spend the night.

And then…maybe something would happen between them. Or not. Probably not.

But then she'd get him to White Plains, he'd give her one last kiss, tell her he'd see her at the picnic, and they would each get on with their lives.

That thought made her feel so sad.

They said goodbye to Danny. The way Micah and Danny hugged each other almost brought tears to her eyes. "I want to work with you again," Micah said, clapping Danny on the back.

"You know where I am," Danny said with his sweet guy smile.

"Thank you," she said to Danny, going in for a hug.

"Be careful," he whispered into her hair. "With him." She leaned back, her arms still around her. "He's not as tough as he pretends and you are…important to him."

And then he stepped away with a big wave, and she and Micah piled into the truck.

She was rattled by Danny's words, not because she didn't believe them. She did. She'd hurt Micah last night with her carelessness. Understanding she had the power to hurt him was heavy. A power she'd never expected to have.

His phone buzzed and he fished it out of his back pocket. "Sorry. I need to take this."

"Of course," she said, and he answered his phone. She pulled out of the parking area and drove down the long drive toward the highway that would take them home.

She only heard one side of the conversation, but it was clearly Jo and she was unhappy with him.

"I…no, Jo…I get it. Of course. Yes…there were a few people. I took some photos. I was…polite…. Well, I can't control what people say on TikTok, Jo…. I don't know, it's the fucking internet…. Jo. Jo. Come on…. You gave him a ride home! Why didn't you give me a ride home? Fine. Yes. Fine. I'm sorry. Yes. Danny is out. Can you call Miguel? …Oh. Thanks. Great…. Yeah. I'll be back for the meeting. I promise. Yes. I promise."

Micah hung up and put his phone in the cupholder in the console between them.

"Why is she mad at you if Alex started the fight?"

"Because I am the one who always finishes it. Like an idiot."

"You should stop doing that," Helen said, and he laughed.

"No shit."

"Have you ever done therapy?" Helen asked.

"Hours of it."

"And it didn't work?"

"Well, the therapist's advice was to not be in a band with my brother." He shrugged. Like that was that.

"Well, I imagine there's more to it than that," she said.

"Like what?"

"Like resist the urge to finish the fights your brother starts? Like when he walks away, you go with him."

"That easy, huh?"

"Actually." She laughed. "Yes. It's just the past that makes it seem hard."

"You get that little nugget in therapy?"

"No. Actually on a notebook I bought in a bookstore. We need to get some gas," she said, glancing down at her gas gauge.

"And coffee."

"Do you mind if I call my family ahead of you coming? My parents will want a chance to put together some kind of red carpet and my aunt will want to make you a meal. She's a Michelin-starred chef, so the food will be amazing. And, I mean, they won't make a big deal, they'll make the usual size deal. But even that's kind of a big deal, but it's also, you know…" She wrinkled her nose. "It's kind of nice."

"Of course. I love a red carpet. So…" he said and then stopped.

"What?"

"Your whole family lives together? Like your aunts and uncles and everything?"

"It's a big property. Everyone has their own house, but yes. We are pretty all together."

"Isn't that…a lot?"

"Sometimes. But most of the time it's amazing."

"Where do you live?" he asked.

She was embarrassed to even say it. "With my parents. I sleep in my childhood bed." She glanced over at him and he put his hands up.

"I'm not judging you," he said.

"It just made sense, after Evan died. I was pregnant and grieving and—"

"Hey," he said, his hand on her knee. "I get it. You were trying to survive, Helen."

But she was past surviving now, wasn't she? And that house was too damn small. She needed her own space, not just a bedroom with a door. But a house. Or maybe an apartment in Catskill.

The one where Dani lived had a pool and a jungle gym. Bea would love it.

They stopped to get gas and coffee, and she walked over to the scrubby grass around the air pump. The highway was just in the distance and there was an empty lot she was staring at full of trash and sunlight. It was one of those edge-of-spring, edge-of-summer days that felt like a song. Like there was nothing but possibility all around.

Maybe she was giddy from the orgasms. Or Micah. Or both. But maybe it was being out in the world again, her life the way it was supposed to be without this last three-year blip. But she felt flush with living. She stretched out her arms, flexed her hands. Alive in her body in a way…she'd forgotten. How was it possible to forget this feeling?

She called Jonah.

"Hey," he said.

"Are you sitting down?"

"No. Do I need to be?"

"Well, you need to be braced."

"I'm braced," he said. She heard her mom's voice in the background and she imagined him putting his hand on her shoulder in their kitchen.

"Micah Sullivan is Michael Bassiter. His mom was Emmaline. He's a Haven House kid." Jonah was silent. She looked at her screen to see if the call dropped. No. He was still there.

"Jonah?"

"You're kidding me."

"I'm not. Remember the kid who sat outside the nurses station for hours—?"

"No!"

"That was Micah." She explained the stepdad and adoption. The nickname.

"And we didn't recognize him," Jonah said.

"Well, I think to be fair to us, those dots are pretty hard to connect. But, and brace yourself again." She heard her mom laugh in the background. "Micah is coming to the inn today," she said. "He's going to stay for dinner."

"Oh my god—"

"No, listen. Everyone needs to try and be cool, okay? This doesn't need to be a whole thing."

"Cool?" Jonah laughed. "You're telling me to be cool. I'm not the one who hid in a closet in White Plains."

"How do you know that?"

"I watched you go into it, dummy. It was one door shy of three doors down and Jo said 'She just went into a closet.' So you don't need to lecture me about playing it cool."

She could be embarrassed or affronted, but honestly, it was only funny. She tipped her head back and laughed.

"Wow," Jonah said. "It's been a while since I've heard that sound."

It had been a while since she'd felt this way. Happy and alive. "Give Bea a hug and tell her I'll be home in two hours."

"You know she doesn't understand time."

"I know," she said. "We gotta get on that."

She got back in the car and Micah was sleeping, slumped against the door, his hat pulled down low. The sun gilded him in a strange way, part spotlight, part Instagram filter, and the blond of his beard glowed gold.

"Stop staring at me," he muttered, the edge of his lush lip curling up.

"Stop being so damn pretty."

He laughed and tucked his hat down a little further. And they drove off, both of them still smiling.

CHAPTER

Twenty~One

MICAH

Except for their arrival at Haven House when he was a kid, he didn't have crystal-clear memories of the place. He didn't remember what they did all day or what they ate. Where they slept.

He remembered being worried.

But now, as they pulled off the small highway onto smaller and smaller roads, he felt as if more stuff was coming back to him. If not memory then…something else. Something slightly more primordial.

"You okay?" Helen asked, looking over at him. Her eyes so serious.

"Sure."

"You're just…you're, like, super still."

The trees were so tall the bright green canopies met over the road and sunlight filtered down in patches. A deer stood at the edge of the road, nose twitching.

"Was there a guy here, a big burly guy? Real quiet but he was always building something—"

"That would be Uncle Max."

"I liked him. He didn't ask me questions and he let me tag along when he was building a fence."

"Uncle Max was always building something. He had a really awful thing happen to him when he was a police officer and he came up here to hide out and heal."

"Building fences worked?"

"Well, it didn't hurt. Then Aunt Delia came along with her daughter, Josie, and did the rest of the hard work." She smiled and then sobered. "He's here. If that means anything to you. You'll see him again."

He felt his heart kind of leap in his chest.

"He won't remember me. I doubt I said two words to him."

They drove past a wooden sign that said Haven House and pulled into the driveway. There was a big yellow farmhouse to his right, and to the left was a series of buildings. The biggest one had a waterslide coming out the top of it, twisting around only to go back into the building at the bottom.

"The water slide sure as shit wasn't here when I was here!"

"It's grown a lot," she said. "We have a kitchen and dorms. We have an art studio and a school building. Fundraising this year is going towards a bigger rec center and, yes, another water slide."

"It's impressive," he said.

"Thank you," she said. She was obviously proud of herself and she should be.

"You want a tour?"

"Is your daughter here?" he asked.

"Yeah, of course. Do you want to meet her?"

"Of course." And as if he'd summoned them, the door to the farmhouse opened and two adults walked out, trying to be cool.

Jonah he recognized. The woman looked just like Helen.

"Here we go," she said and threw open her car door just as a little girl pushed through all those grown ups' legs and came running down the stairs in pink tennis shoes with her black curls bouncing.

Helen's daughter.

Helen

"Bea!" she shouted and ran to scoop up her little girl, who wrapped her arms and legs around Helen's body and squeezed tight. Helen had been busy the last 48 hours, and somehow completely outside of her life, so the way she would usually miss her daughter had taken a back seat to bailing a rock star out of jail and then making out with him at a cabin in northern New York. But now that she had her little girl back in her arms she was sick with missing her. Weak with it.

"How are you sweetie?" she asked, kissing and kissing and kissing her. "I missed you so much."

"Do you want to hear what I did?" Bea asked and Helen nodded, even though she knew what she was in for. The rambling three-year-old monologue that would be half a story about her day and half a story about a dream she'd had interspersed with a play-by-play of *Paw Patrol*.

She let her family handle Micah and she soaked her little girl up through her skin.

"Mama," Bea said, finally taking a breath. "Who is that?"

She pointed, and Helen turned to find Micah shaking Mom's hand. A shaft of afternoon sunlight hit his bracelets and the ring on his thumb. The gold in the tips of his hair. He looked like a character in a fantasy novel, dipped in gold. Full of magic.

And while Jonah talked to him, he was looking at her. Watching her. His face was shadowed by the baseball cap he wore so she couldn't see his expression, but she could feel his attention. It had been the same way when they were in that bunkie together.

All of his attention, his creativity, his not-insignificant amount of charisma, focused like a laser—on her.

Like she was the only thing in the world.

Oh God, she thought.

It was disconcerting and flattering. And...exciting. To be the thing he focused on. He was just a man, sure. But he was a man who created her favorite songs. A man who captivated stadiums of people.

Who captivated her.

And she was falling for him. Not like in love, that would be ridiculous. But falling for this feeling. This life of glitter and charm. Him.

Shit. It wasn't love but it was infatuation, maybe?

"That's Micah," Helen told Bea, walking back over to him. The closer they got, the softer Micah's face went, until, by the time they were standing next to him, he was smiling.

"Micah," she said. "This is my daughter, Bea." She gave Bea a little jostle in her arms and she laughed. "Bea this is Micah."

"Micah is a kind of stone," Bea said.

"It is," Micah said, his eyes going wide. Bea had been obsessed with a gem book a month ago. She'd retained a weird amount of it.

"It's shiny."

"That's what I've heard."

"I have a turtle."

"Do you?"

"And a dog. The turtle is upstairs but Kiwi is here..."

"No." Helen tried to stop the inevitable. "Bea. Don't."

"Kiwi!" Bea shouted, and from around the edge of the building came the four dogs, barking and tail wagging, and once they realized there was stranger, the four of them, each a total failure as a guard dog, began jumping on poor Micah. Micah crouched down, petting their heads, getting drowned by dog slobber.

All while Bea introduced him to each of them.

"Bingo eats poop," Bea said about their chocolate Lab mix. "And sometimes he throws it up and eats it again."

"Oh my god." Mom moaned like she was dying inside.

Micah pushed Bingo's licking face away and got to his feet.

"Is there any way to get a tour?" he asked. "Helen has been blackmailing me every step of our journey, so I think at this point I'm donating half my life to Haven House."

"She was always a tough negotiator," Jonah said, his arm over her shoulders. "And I'd love to give you a tour."

"Me too!" Bea said and reached up and grabbed both their hands. Helen found herself with a lump in her throat so big she couldn't speak.

"You do that," Daphne said, looping her arm through Helen's. "And when you're done we'll meet you over at the inn."

Jonah and Bea led Micah away and Helen immediately started shaking her head. "Don't, Mom. Don't say a word."

"Well, that's not going to happen. I will say one thing and then I'm going to play it so cool for the rest of the night you won't even believe it's me."

"What's your one thing?"

"The way that man just looked at you, honey?" Daphne opened her eyes up wide. "I mean…"

Part of Helen wanted to go *I know, right? Can you believe it?*

Part of her just wanted to settle right down deep in the thrill of the whole thing.

But that wasn't smart. That was, in fact, completely dangerous. Her heart had been broken so badly it had changed her. She wasn't interested in more of that. And infatuation with Micah Sullivan was a surefire way to get hurt. She could feel it happening already. The infatuation and the hurt.

"Mom." Helen wrapped her arms around her mom, who wrapped her own arms around Helen. "That's what he does, you know. He…creates connection. He makes everyone feel important to him. He's a rock star. It's part of the job."

"I don't know, Helen," Mom said. "That look…"

"Is the same look on album covers," Helen said and leaned back. "I'm not special. *He's* special and that whole charisma thing is part of it. Please, trust me. Let that little twinkle in your eye go."

For me, she thought, *because it's hard enough to be reasonable on my own.*

Daphne sighed and blew out a long breath. "I think you're special."

"Thanks, Mom. And thanks for taking care of Bea for me."

"My pleasure. Anytime. Come on, let's go over to the inn and help Alice. She was threatening to make the rock star peel potatoes."

Micah

"I'm sorry we didn't recognize you," Jonah said. They were walking a trail from Haven House to the inn. The tour had been extensive and impressive. Bea was in front of them with the dogs.

"How could you? I was a kid," Micah said, fully realizing it had been ridiculous for him to get upset over it.

"How is your mom?" Jonah asked, stepping wide around a puddle.

"She died a few years ago."

"Oh, Micah, I'm sorry to hear that. She was so young."

"Yeah. Cervical cancer. It was fast."

"That must have been difficult."

Micah stepped over a big boulder and ducked under a thorny bush growing into the trail. "It all happened just when the band took off," Micah said. "And I think she downplayed everything that was going on with her so that I could enjoy what was happening to me. By the time she told me, it was too late for anything to be done."

"I remember your mom," Jonah said. "When she was here. Everything she was trying to do was for you. To make a better life for you."

Micah blew out a hard breath. "I know. And she did."

Jonah clapped a hand on Micah's back and he had to blink back tears.

The trail opened up and they stood on a little rise overlooking a lodge and a dozen cabins. A larger cabin was at their right. And another at their left.

"Wow," Micah said. "Helen said you all lived near each other and I can totally see why. It's beautiful."

"My brother and father built this place with their own hands, and it's a long dramatic story but we didn't know each other for most of our lives. When I finally did meet my brothers and my father and got over what I thought had been done to my mother and I—all I wanted was for our families to be in each other's lives. The Riverview Inn has been a dream."

"Did your parents live here?"

"They did. We had some really good years here all together as a family. But Mom died at the beginning of the pandemic and Dad died a week after her."

"Jonah," he said. "I'm so sorry."

"Thank you. You know," Jonah said. "For a guy with such a shit reputation, you're not so bad."

Micah stepped down onto a granite rock, heading toward the lodge, but Jonah put a hand on his shoulder, stopping him.

"The new album, it's about Helen, isn't it?" Jonah asked.

Stunned, Micah turned and nearly tripped on the edge of the stone he was standing on.

"How did you know?"

"You read that article in the *New York Times*."

"I did," Micah said, the words coming out of his mouth like they were escaping. Glad to finally be out.

Jonah crossed his arms over his chest. His hands were in fists and Micah stepped back realizing Jonah was angry.

"Helen had her mother and me read her victim impact statement a million times, and some of those lines are seared into my brain. *Hurting you won't change a thing. Hurting you won't ease my pain.* Those are her words. *Exactly.*"

"They are," Micah admitted. "I was…in a dark place at the beginning of the pandemic, and when I read that article, I was just inspired by how brave she was. How selfless."

"What about White Knuckled?" Jonah asked. Another song Micah had written based on that victim statement. *These white-knuckle nights are too long. It's me and the ghosts until dawn.*

Micah nodded.

"Jesus," Jonah muttered, and the shame Micah had been rationalizing made him sick. "Have you told her?"

Micah shook his head.

"If she finds out on her own she's going to feel betrayed. She hates pity—"

"I don't pity her."

"Your pity for her is all over those songs," Jonah snapped. "The way you take her devastation and reduce it to a three-minute harmony. You plagiarized her words. You mined her pain."

The words hit him hard. So hard he was speechless.

"I won't hurt her."

"You called her in the middle of the night to bail you out of jail," Jonah said, his voice clipped but low so Bea couldn't hear him. "You've got a reputation for a short temper and violence. I know the worst moment in her life is going to make you fucking rich. So, you'll forgive me for calling bullshit on that."

"I will pay her."

Oh. That had been the wrong thing to say. He knew it even as it came out of his mouth.

"That…I'm sorry," he said.

"I know it's not fair and maybe I'm talking out my ass, but I'm her father and I won't see her hurt anymore, Micah. You should leave her alone." Jonah walked past him. "Wait for me, Bea," he shouted and caught up to his granddaughter.

As far as warning conversations from fathers went, it had been extremely effective. He couldn't argue. There was nothing to say in his own defense that didn't sound childish. He pulled his phone out of his pocket and called Jo.

"Hey," he said. "Can you send a car to get me?"

"Where?"

He gave her the address.

"Now?"

Jonah didn't want to hurt Helen either, and leaving right now would hurt her. And he owed her truth.

"Dawn."

SOMEHOW, ten minutes later, he was peeling potatoes in the industrial kitchen of the inn surrounded by what seemed like seven million Mitchells.

"Look at you," Alice said, looking over his shoulder as he made short work of the potatoes. "You've done this before."

"My first job was in a kitchen," he said. He set down the peeler and looked at the heap of potatoes on the acrylic cutting board. "You want me to cut them?"

"Julienne? But big?"

"Sure. You're making fries?"

"Bea created the menu, so fries it is."

A big guy came into the kitchen, wiping his hands on a towel.

"Hey," Alice said, turning from the stove. "Max meet Micah. Micah, Max."

Max was a big guy, dark hair. He was the kind of guy who, even when he was completely silent, was somehow the loudest guy in the room. He just had weight—and in the whole of Helen's family, all the men had weight and gravitas. But Max was something special.

"Hi," Max said and came up and shook Micah's hand.

"Hi. Nice to meet you. Thanks for having me in your home."

"We've met before, though, right?" Max squinted at him, his head turned like he was trying to see him clearly.

"I was a kid. I doubt you—"

"You helped me build the fence at the edge of Haven House when it first opened. You were real quiet. I liked that about you."

Delia, the redhead came in with some teenagers. Max slung his arm around his wife's neck and kissed her forehead.

"Yeah," Micah said, stupidly pleased someone remembered him. "That was me."

"Not so quiet anymore. I loved that duet you did with Brandi Carlile."

Max grabbed a beer from the fridge and offered Micah one.

"No thanks," he said. Max pulled up a stool.

"How is the tour prep going?" Delia asked.

The kitchen door opened again and it was Helen and Daphne coming in, Jonah behind them. It seemed everyone was suddenly in the kitchen.

"We've got lots of time. Two months until we open at Madison Square Garden, so we're still working out some kinks."

"I love the new album," one of the teenagers said, in a great rush. She was bright pink with dark hair and she looked so much like Max that she could only be his kid. He just couldn't remember the name. There were so many teenagers.

"Thank you."

"Did you really write the whole thing during the pandemic?"

"I did."

"Those live Instagrams you did were smoking hot," another teenage girl said, and there was a riot of giggles and Jonah turned and gave them solid glares.

"Well," Delia, under Max's arm, shrugged. "They were."

"It was kind of the point," Micah said.

"Was it hard?" a boy asked. This kid looked like a linebacker but he had the mullet of a hockey player. "Writing an album by yourself, in lockdown and everything?"

Micah felt Jonah's stare and Helen standing unaware. Saying it now, here, in front of everyone didn't seem right.

"It was actually easier than it's ever been," Micah answered truthfully. "I think because there weren't any distractions. I just wrote and played music. It's weird, and I know it was awful for a lot of people and I come from a place of privilege, but for me the lockdown wasn't too bad."

The teenagers jumped into a conversation about who'd had it worse during the lockdown, and the argument flowed around the room, people chiming in and calling people out. Everyone laughing. No one took the argument seriously.

Micah realized how amazing this was, the way all the kids were talking and the parents weren't having to bridge all the gaps. No one had their phones out, either. It spoke of a place where everyone felt safe. Trusted. No one was checking the temperature of the undercurrents.

He'd been checking the undercurrents his whole life.

He wished, in a way, that his mother could have been alive to see this. When they'd driven up here in the Datsun, she'd wanted something like this. For both him and Alex.

And they got a version of it, but meaner. Colder. Transactional.

I wish my brother was here to see this.

I wish my mother was.

"All right!" Alice said and clapped her hands. She'd been tirelessly working the fryer while her husband, Gabe, had been out at a charcoal grill with steaks. "Kids, set the table. Pour water. Dinner is ready."

The teenagers, in very un-teenager-like behavior, jumped to do what she asked and Bea, who'd been sitting next to him as quality control, soaking the potatoes, took his hand. "We do water," she said. And he was pulled into the next room, which was huge.

A dining room occupied the area in front of the tall windows. Tables had been pushed together and tablecloths stretched over them. There were at least a dozen chairs squeezed around the makeshift table. Down a few steps was a spacious living room, with big couches and chairs and two fireplaces. There were four dogs flopped around on the floor.

All I need is this home. These dogs. My girl. A cold beer…

He pulled out the piece of paper and the pen from his shirt pocket and wrote down the lyric.

"Is he…writing a song right in front of us?" Delia asked Helen in a voice that carried through the big room and they all looked at him.

"You get used to it," Helen said and winked at him.

He'd had a glimpse of this when he was young and had been chasing it ever since. Family.

But he'd put it together through a distorted lens. His stepfather's scraps of affection and baseline tolerance hadn't been love. Protecting his brother and taking responsibility for the shit he pulled wasn't love either.

He thought of his mother and the way she'd compromised everything for security. Including him.

That was such a difficult kind of love.

"Hey, rock star," Alice said. He liked Alice. His fame meant absolutely nothing to her. "We're waiting on you."

He realized everyone was sitting and beautiful slices of steak were being handed out along with big platters of frites and Caesar salad. And the middle of it was Helen. Safe and secure. Loved.

I love her, he thought, the words coming out of the fog. This feeling he had, this inspiration, this compelled obsession, he'd been pretending it wasn't love. But he couldn't lie about it anymore.

He loved her.

And he was where he should be. On the outside.

"Coming."

CHAPTER
Twenty~Three

Helen

Bea fell asleep in Helen's arms at the table, something she hadn't done in a really long time. Though it had been a long time since the family had lingered at the table like this. Even on Sundays, dinners were a faster affair.

But tonight, Micah was telling stories and everyone was asking questions, and another bottle of wine had been opened and another pot of tea made, and Bea had climbed into Helen's lap, put her head on her shoulder and fallen asleep.

Helen was so reluctant to leave. So reluctant to stop holding this usually squirming bundle of energy. So reluctant to leave the warm glow of this table.

But then her hand fell asleep. And her arm.

And Bea started snoring.

The party, for her anyway, was over.

"I'm going to get Bea in bed," she said to her mom, who was sitting next to her.

"You need help?"

"No. You, my mother, have done enough." She leaned over

and kissed Daphne's cheek. "I'm going to put him in the big cabin," Daphne whispered. "Just so you know."

"I'm going to get her home," she said to Micah, ignoring her booty call-arranging mother.

"Do you need some help?" he asked, rising half out of his seat.

"No," she said. "It's a whole thing. She's going to wake up at some point and then I'm going to have to read some stories and listen to some stories and there will be cuddling. It's a one-man job."

"Of course," he said. Her whole family watched as he rounded the table toward her, and her heart was beating hard against her chest, against her daughter's chest and her own little heartbeat.

And it felt like she was on some kind of loop. Wanting him and dying a little bit the closer he came.

"I'll walk you out," he said, standing at the door to the kitchen. And still her family watched. Some playing it cool. Some, her mother being the worst of them, staring with hearts in their eyes.

Don't, she wanted to say. Don't get excited. Don't get me excited. This isn't the start of something. It's the end.

They walked through the kitchen, where the teenagers were not cleaning up, but instead sitting around the kitchen with their phones out.

"Don't you dare take pictures," Helen said to each of them as they walked by.

"Pictures of what?" Stella asked, and she wasn't even being sarcastic.

Micah laughed, holding open the back door to the kitchen. "Man, I got real boring real fast."

"Don't take it personally."

Outside the moon was waxing, just above the dark shadows of the trees. And stars were visible beneath dark clouds. The night was cool and she held her daughter a little closer. The gravel crunched under their feet, the only sound between them.

What do I do? How do I say goodbye? Is this, like...over? No, she thought, suddenly relieved to remember the picnic. *I'll see him again.* But then she chastised herself for weird, wishful thinking.

"Wow," he said. "I can practically hear you thinking."

"I'm just…it's been a wild few days, you know?"

"I know." He glanced around at all the cars. "Which one has the car seat in it?"

Oh, he was a sweet guy. He really was. She pointed at her mom's car, the gray SUV with Farmers Feed Cities bumper sticker. He held open the back door and she bent to put Bea in her car seat. She protested, grumpily, her curls all over her face. Helen clipped her in and then brushed her hair away, kissing her forehead. Bea fell right back to sleep.

She stood up and faced Micah, the steel of the door between them.

"I need to tell you something," he said.

"So do I," she said, leaning against the door. "Can I go first? Otherwise, I'll never say it."

"Yeah," he said, subdued in the moonlight. "Go ahead."

"There's no way you would have known this when you called me to get you out of jail, but it was exactly what I needed. I was stuck, Micah. I was stuck and I was scared, and you pushed me right back into living. I'd sort of resigned myself to just being that woman whose fiancé died in that crash. And the woman who forgave the driver that killed him and Bea's mom and Jonah and Daphne's daughter. I was surviving in pieces, and you came along and put me back together."

There'd been thousands of words written about his face and she'd read a lot of them. His serious eyes. His lush mouth. The bad-boy scar. But in person he was so much more. He was more than his looks. More than his music. More than his band. More than his complicated relationship with his brother.

She reached up and touched the scar on his face, her fingertip tracing the raised, jagged line.

"Did it hurt?" she asked. He nodded.

"Was it scary?" He nodded again.

"And now everyone just thinks it's sexy," she said.

The world saw him in pieces, too.

She saw the whole of him.

He pulled her around the door and then shut it, quietly. He leaned back against the car and settled her body against his. She took a breath, and then he did, and they were working in tandem. Fuck, this intimacy she'd been so scared of, now she craved it. Wanted it with every part of her body.

"I've texted Jo," he said, his voice a low murmur, his eyes on hers and then dipping to her mouth and then up to the pile of hair on her head, and she got the sense that he was memorizing her the same way she was memorizing him.

He, too, was already saying goodbye.

"She's sending a car to get me at six tomorrow morning."

"Really?" She couldn't hide her disappointment and then felt ridiculous. "Of course," she said and attempted to step back, but he didn't let go. "You have so much to get back to."

Nothing had to be strange about this except for the way her body was going berserk. She wanted to kiss him. She wanted to taste him. Hold him tight. Pull off those clothes and run her hands over his body the way he'd run his over hers the previous night. She wanted every pleasure he'd given her to be returned in kind.

She wanted him. Badly.

And holding all that desire in her body and not doing anything about it was hard. She felt like all her wiring was wrong. She trembled in the cool air against his warm body, clutching her self-control and self-respect.

And then he kissed her. His hands spread wide against her back, his fingertips pressing against her clothes and into her skin until she was flush against him. She gasped and he swept his tongue into her mouth. Consuming her. And she moaned, high and wild, clutching him to her.

It wasn't a kiss, it was a fevered goodbye. It was a painful wish. It was restraint and abandon and she was dizzy with want.

He tore his mouth away, pressed his forehead against hers.

"Christ, Helen," he breathed. "I want you."

"I want you, too."

But her daughter was in the car. And there wasn't anywhere for this desire to go. And she was just coming back to herself. And he had a whole life to get back to. A band and a tour and Madison Square Garden.

Reason swept in.

"I have to go," she finally forced herself to say. And then she forced herself to step back. Her hands slid over his shirt, memorizing the feel of his muscles and bones. "My daughter."

"Of course." He stepped back too. Giving her all the room she needed.

"Don't forget the picnic," she said, and he laughed.

"I can't remember where we landed with all that blackmail. I think I'm setting up chairs?"

She laughed, but she felt like crying. "I'll send you an email."

"And you have my number."

Yeah. She did. She had Micah Sullivan's number.

She opened the driver-side door. The keys, as the family had grown used to doing over the years so people could move cars and leave when they needed, were tucked under the mat.

She pressed her hand to the window and he smiled. And maybe she was flattering herself but she thought he looked sad too. Sad she was leaving. That this was over.

And then, because her daughter was sleeping in the back and her life pulled her ever forward, she drove away.

As predicted, Bea woke up on the stairs going up to her bedroom.

"Mama?" she said in her sleepy little-girl voice that sent a thunderbolt of tenderness right through Helen.

"Yeah, sweetie," she whispered into her ear.

"Potty."

They took a detour into the dark bathroom and Helen helped her daughter take down her pants and sit on the toilet.

"Cold seat," Bea said with a little shiver dance.

"I missed you," Helen said when they were done and Bea had washed her hands and her face. They walked into Bea's bedroom and Helen kept the light off while tucking her into bed.

"Mama stay," Bea whispered, and the words weren't even out of her mouth before Helen was crawling in next to her daughter. "Story."

"Sure," Helen said, reaching for the stack of books by the bed. She got halfway through *The Naughty Bunny* before Bea fell asleep, curled in against her.

For three years her body had stopped being her own. It had been a vessel for Bea, and for grief. And then it had been a rampaging forest fire of hormones and then a source of food and comfort for a baby. She'd been touched more in these three years than any other time in her life. And there'd been moments she'd wished she could just lie, naked and cold and untouched in the middle of her bed for, like, a week. But that feeling didn't last long.

Carefully, inch by inch, she pulled away from her daughter, who rolled—sighing and snoring—into the place Helen left behind.

She lay at the edge of the bed and stared up at the ceiling. The faint glow in the dark stars that had lost most of their glow about a year ago.

I should really take those down, she thought. It was somewhere in the middle of her gigantic to-do list. She took her phone out of her back pocket and set it on her chest.

Her heart was beating beneath her ribs. Her blood pounding through her body.

Micah Sullivan was leaving tomorrow morning. And this whole…departure from her regular life would be over. It felt, not to be dramatic, that tonight was the last chance at something.

Even if that something was a one-night stand.

But something had started in that closet in White Plains. And it would be wrong not to finish it.

Look at me rationalizing sex.

She crept out of Bea's bed and stood in the dark shadows of the hallway. Downstairs she could hear her parents talking. She took a deep breath and did something she'd never done before and imagined she might never do again.

Booty-called a rock star.

She put a hand over her mouth to smother the hysterical laughter.

You awake? she texted.

Immediately the three dots showed up.

Cabin nine, he texted. *Come over.*

There, she thought, breathless and wild. There. It's done. It's happening.

CHAPTER

Twenty-Four

MICAH

He showered but didn't have anything clean to wear so he used the thick robe that hung in the closet and felt like Burt Reynolds in every cheesy 70s movie. His phone buzzed and he half expected it to be Helen telling him she wasn't going to come. That she'd changed her mind.

He'd been hoping for the *You awake?* text from her, but thought the odds were pretty stacked against him.

This was a text from his brother.

When you coming back was all it said.

Tomorrow? He texted back. *Why?*

I can't just miss you?

You in trouble? he texted and there was no answer. And this was the part of their story where Micah would put on his pants and go looking for his brother. Following the crumbs until he found him on the edge of some disaster. And then Micah would pull him back by his shirt and jump in for him.

I'm not doing it anymore, he thought. And not just because a beautiful woman was coming to this well-appointed cottage. But because he couldn't do it anymore. *I'm sorry, Mom,* he thought. *But I can't keep doing this. It doesn't work. And I deserve more.*

He turned his phone off. Tossed it onto his pile of dirty clothes in the corner just as there was a knock at the door. His dick twitched against his robe as he crossed the room. Outside, Helen stood in a shaft of clear blue moonlight. It silvered her, made her skin glow and the shadows around her mysterious. She looked otherworldly. And he was a rock star; there'd been more than a few beautiful women in his life, but none like her. None with her gravitas and heartache and hope.

She was a song he wished he was good enough to write.

"You want to come in?" he asked after a long second, and she stepped in and he shut the door behind her.

"You want—"

"I don't want to talk," she said.

Yeah. I can get behind that.

He took one gliding step toward her, his hands cupping her face, pulling her to him. She grabbed his wrists like there was a storm and he was the only thing keeping her standing. He put everything he felt into that kiss. The wonder and the desire, and it was messy and wild and she met him with her own ferociousness. He abandoned her cheeks for her waist, picking her up and spinning to push her against the door. She moaned into his mouth, fitting her body against his like they'd done this a million times.

She wrapped her legs around his waist and her hands pushed the robe off his shoulders. Blood thundered through his body down to his dick. He arched against her and she moaned again— god, he loved that sound—pushing back into him.

Her skirt had flipped up when she lifted her legs around his waist and it was just his dick against what felt like damp, silky underwear. He pushed, sliding against it, finding the sweet dip between her legs.

She leaned back against the door, her hands running over his chest. The stupid tattoo he got when he and Alex were eighteen;

the much better tattoo he got when he had some money and some sense.

Her thumb brushed his painfully hard nipple and he gasped. Her eyes, wide and curious, narrowed with intent and she pressed harder with her nail, her eyes watching him, gauging his response.

He ran his hands along her thighs, under that skirt to her ass, which he squeezed with both hands, his fingers slipping under the elastic of that silky underwear.

"Yes," she whimpered, her breath hitching and breaking.

Every reaction of hers went through him like a thunderbolt, magnified and hot. And he didn't know how to tell her they needed to slow down. That he wanted to make this good for her, but he was raw and losing it. He was a full-grown man, a fucking rock star. And he felt like a boy in front of her.

He stepped back, and her legs slipped to the floor.

A breath, he thought, just a breath to get himself under control. But she shoved the rest of the robe off his body and he stood there naked. So naked.

Almost too naked. Her eyes taking in every inch of him. And he felt all at once how he hadn't been totally truthful with her. And he'd exerted some of his star power on her to get her to pick him up and go to Danny's, and yet he didn't know how to reconcile this moment.

He was so powerless in front of her.

And then she reached down and cupped his dick. Her fingers soft but not light. She bit her lip, looking at him through her lashes and he almost lost it right there. Slowly, she stroked him. Her thumb over the top, where precome he could not control oozed out of him. Again, she did it. Both hands. One cupping his balls, the other jacking him. He grabbed her face, his fingers tangling in her hair, bringing her close to him. The plan was to kiss her, kiss her senseless. Kiss her like he needed her to breathe. But she squeezed just right. Just perfect and he gasped. Shaking. Pressing his head to hers.

"Yes," he whispered. Breathing her in, breathing her out.

"I want…"

"Yes," he whispered.

And then she was slipping onto her knees in front of him. And he dared not look down. It would be over if he looked down. It would be as close to a sexual disaster as he'd gotten in years if he looked down.

He looked down.

And she was so pretty, her hair around her shoulders. Her eyes intent. Her face so serious. And then she leaned forward and licked him. Slipped her lips over him. Her breath hot, her mouth so wet and tight.

He stared up at the ceiling. Ever sense completely wrapped up in her. She hummed in her throat, a happy little sound that made him insane for her. For more of her. All of her.

Don't look down.

He looked down.

He'd lived every fantasy only to realize they were empty. Shallow. But this, her on her knees in front of him, loving this as much as he was…, it was so real it hurt. It pierced him.

He stepped back and she fell forward a little catching herself on his legs. There were a thousand things he could do, pick her up and put her down on the bed being top of the list, but even that was too much. He was down on his knees on the rug with her, his hand pulling her shirt over her head. Slipping beneath the skirt to find her wet and hot.

"I can't," he breathed into her mouth. *Wait. Stand it. Imagine tomorrow.*

"Me neither."

He reached for the wallet he'd taken out of his back pocket before his shower—when he'd been a cooler and calmer version of himself—and put on his bed, thinking about this moment but it in a more abstract way. Not knowing how ravenous he'd be. How crazed.

Pulling his fingers away from her body was like going into the cold after being in a sauna, but the condom wrapper wasn't going to open itself. Without his hand distracting her, she bent forward again, her lips over his cock, and he hissed and fought for control and finally had to push her away just so he could keep his wits about him.

She lay back on the rug, her hair wild around her. She wore a black bra with a little bit of lace and it was—relatively speaking—a tiny bit sexy. But on her it was a knockout punch. She licked her hand while he watched and wrapped her fingers around his dick again.

"You're making me crazy."

"Good," she whispered. "I like you crazy."

Finally, he got the condom open and knocked her hand out of the way so he could slip it on. He reached under that skirt and pulled off her underwear. He tossed it toward the corner with his dirty clothes. And he got down between her legs, there on the floor, at the edge of his willpower.

He didn't like looking women in the eye when he slid inside of them. He feared what his face would reveal, and he was scared of what her face would reveal, and the intimacy was just too much.

But he caught Helen's eye and there was no looking away.

There was no protecting himself or hiding.

It was them and moonlight and a moment so profound he could only live in it.

Her eyes went wide and her chin arched up, her neck long and graceful in the moonlight. He slid his hand over it, felt the pulse of her heart against his fingers, the heat of her skin. She was tight. So tight he worried he might hurt her. And he was careful, and it took two lifetimes to do it, but he was finally deep inside of her.

He dropped his head against her chest. Kissed the rise of her breast, pulled her nipple into his mouth through the lace of her bra.

She hissed and arched into him, her hips shifting. Fucking him without fucking him and he pressed his head into her harder. Holding her there. Holding himself there.

"Micah," she breathed. Twisting against him. "Please."

His control shattered and he started fucking into her. Tiny little movements because he couldn't stand sliding out of her. Didn't want to lift his body away from hers. It was excruciating bliss.

This wasn't going to last long, so he slipped his fingers between them to help her over. But her fingers were already there, working her clit, and suddenly *that* he wanted to see. Needed to see.

He sat back on his knees, pulled her up closer. One hand braced on her stomach, the other on her knee.

She stopped as if suddenly embarrassed that he was watching.

"No," he said. "It's so beautiful. Keep going."

"I'm gonna—" She gulped as she stroked herself. Hard and fast.

"Me too."

He felt her squeeze him. A red flush crawled up from her chest, across her neck to her face. A scream got strangled in her throat and she clutched at him. Pulling him into her as she came against him. They were locked together on that floor, without boundaries or sense. They were something that never should have happened and somehow felt inevitable all at the same time.

Twenty~Five

ONCE HE COULD FEEL his body again, he became aware that he was pushing her into the rug with all of his weight. He began to pull away, but she wouldn't let him go. "Stay," she whispered. "Just…a little longer."

He tried to brace his weight so he wasn't on top of her, but she wrapped her arms and legs around him and held on.

"I don't want to squish you," he said into her hair.

"I just want to feel you everywhere for one more minute."

How could he argue? He gave her more weight, not all of it, but enough to feel her hip bones. "You just feel so good," she whispered. And he nodded.

You feel very right.

He bit back the words because this was a goodbye scene. Not the start of something.

Hurting you won't change a thing.

She'd said it herself, and then he'd stolen the words from her.

"I'll be right back." He held the condom and got to his feet, feeling like his muscles were made of rubber bands and his brain was full of sparks. He shut the bathroom door behind him and turned on the light. He got rid of the condom, pissed, washed his hands, splashed water on his face.

Tell her, he said to his reflection. *Just tell her.* It was time.

He could make a million donations to Haven House. His portion of the profit that band made. He would tell her this was how he processed things. He took in pain and turned it into music —but that made him sound like an asshole. He would tell her she inspired him.

And that he was sorry.

And that he hoped that maybe instead of this being the end of something, they could turn it into the beginning of something else.

I love you. I know it seems fast but it also feels like fate. I love you and I think you love me too.

But when he walked back into the bedroom she was gone.

<h1 style="text-align:center">CHAPTER
Twenty-Six</h1>

THE NEXT DAY, she called in sick to Haven House and spent the day with Bea.

She was exhausted and raw in a way that could only be helped by time spent off her phone, away from her computer and deep into the kind of absolutely present state of mind that being with her daughter required.

She didn't want to talk about Micah. She didn't want to think about him. She didn't want to process the last two days. Maybe, in time, she'd get her head around it, but right now she couldn't do it.

They went for a long walk on the trails behind the inn and watched honeybees in the clover Alice had planted in the hopes of starting a honeybee colony. They ate jam sandwiches by the fire pit and played one hundred rounds of Slap Jack at toddler speed.

"I win," Bea said, flopping back onto the rug in her bedroom. "I'm tired, Mommy."

"Yeah? Me too," she said, and crawled over on her knees and flopped down next to Bea.

"Why are you tired?" Bea asked, rolling onto her side and tucking her hands under her cheek like she was in some kind of commercial for girl talk. Charmed and deeply in love with her daughter, Helen did the same.

"I didn't sleep very well," she said.

"Did you count the sheep?"

"I did," she said and brushed her daughter's curls back off her face. "Bea?"

"Yeah."

And suddenly, Helen was here. At this conversation. And she hadn't planned it or expected it. She hadn't created a speech, but in the day with her daughter, the back of her brain had been chewing this up, getting it ready for the right moment. Which apparently was this one.

"How would you feel if we…lived someplace else?"

"Like the moon?" Bea asked with wide eyes.

Helen laughed. "No, like an apartment. Like Daniella and her daughter."

"Oh," Bea said. "I like that pool."

Daniella's apartment had a pool and a playground. It was beyond family friendly.

"We would go by ourselves," she said, giving Bea the whole picture. "No Grandma and Grandpa."

Bea's face crumpled. "Who makes dinner?"

"Me."

"Oh, Mommy, no." Bea wrinkled her nose.

Helen laughed. "Do you want to make dinner?"

"We can go to McDonald's."

"Would you miss Grandma and Grandpa?" Helen asked carefully.

"We would never come back? To visit?"

"No, we'd visit a lot. And they can visit us."

"Grandma doesn't like McDonald's."

"No." Helen laughed again. "She doesn't. We'll have to figure out something else for dinner when she comes."

Bea yawned and Helen realized she might be able to convince her three-year-old to take a rare nap. "You want to go lie down in my bed?" Mommy's bed was a big treat, reserved for sick days and those mornings after Josie was in town and she and Helen had had too much wine.

Bea nodded so Helen got to her feet and pulled her daughter up into her arms. The apartment thing wasn't decided. It was only the first conversation of probably many, but as far as first conversations went, that could not have gone better.

It was funny, she thought as she curled up in her single bed, like a parenthesis around her daughter. Her life had changed once, in a terrible instant. It had torn in half fast and without warning. And she realized, three years later, that if she wanted it to change again, she couldn't count on fate knocking on her door. She had to do it. All on her own. One grueling and unsure step at a time.

Micah

They were all walking around a little aimlessly, waiting for Miguel to show up in White Plains. The band did not do well with waiting. Or boredom. In the corner Sean was flipping cards onto his drum set, trying to flip them hard enough to make noise.

"Hey," Alex said, approaching Micah where he sat on a folding chair in the far corner of the room, resisting the phone in his back pocket with everything in him.

"What?" Micah said.

"Well, you're a little ray of sunshine this morning," Alex said, handing him a cup of coffee.

"Fuck off."

"What happened to you?" Alex asked. "The good girl charity case dump you?"

Micah stood. "Hey! Hey!" Alex laughed, hands up, getting in front of him so he couldn't walk away. "Holy shit, okay. I get it. No jokes about Helen."

Micah sat back down. "Honestly, someone should punch you."

"You've been saying that for years," Alex said. All no harm, no foul. "You all right though? You haven't been yourself since you got back from your little field trip."

Alex sat down next to him in another folding chair and stretched his legs out beside Micah's.

Before every tour, a stylist came in and they discussed their "look" for the tour. It always seemed like bullshit to him, but he'd realized looking around at all the big acts—they had looks. It was a whole curated thing.

And now, both of them were wearing their boots from the last tour. Beaten up and worn down from hours on stage. He craved Helen because she was authentic and here he was, a fraud.

"You…you really like her?" Alex asked quietly. All the teasing was gone from his voice and Micah turned to look at him, waiting for the punch line. But Alex was serious and subdued. He wore a red flannel shirt and he looked so much like their mother it kind of hurt.

"Yeah. I really like her."

"It's not just like that obsessive thing you were doing after you read her article?" he asked. "It's just a question, don't bite my head off. Because you get like this sometimes."

"Like what?"

"Obsessed."

"You know every time I get obsessed it works out pretty well for you."

They were sitting in this rehearsal space because when he was sixteen he'd gotten obsessed with playing the guitar and Alex, always following in his footsteps, started playing too.

And then he got obsessed with writing songs.

And that led to the open mic nights, just the two of them, playing his original songs. And then he'd wanted a band, and then he wanted a better band and here they were.

"Do you honestly think I don't know that?" Alex asked without taking any offense. "So where is she?"

"You were right. I complicate things. I made it harder than it needed to be." Micah shrugged, like it was no big deal, like his heart hadn't been broken in that cabin. "She's not for me."

"I'm sorry, man."

Micah looked at his brother, surprised by the show of empathy.

"What?" he asked defensively. "I can be a nice guy."

"You just choose not to most of the time?" Micah asked with a smile.

"I don't know, you're out there being nice enough for the two of us."

"That's why you didn't like Danny?" Micah asked. "He threw off the nice guy ratio?"

"That guy was beyond nice. You know the road would have chewed him up and spit him out."

Jo came in at that moment, with two gigantic men absolutely made of muscle walking in behind her. "Who are those guys?" Alex asked.

"No idea."

But Jo saw them sitting on the edge of the stage and walked over, the mountain men following.

"I got a bad feeling about this," Alex said.

"Yeah, me too."

"Jo," Alex started. "I don't—"

She held up a hand. "Stop talking," she said. "This is coming from the label so there's no room to bullshit. These are Ivan and Dimitri Shapapalov and they are your new bodyguards. You don't go anywhere without them. That includes dive bars, strip clubs—"

"Who is going to strip clubs?" Micah asked.

"Me," Alex whispered.

"No two-day field trips." Jo eyed Micah. "This brother bullshit between you is going to mess up this band and this tour. I'm not having it."

Well. Babysitter/bodyguards. *It's come to this.* And he wasn't even mad about it.

"I agree with you," Micah said, and his brother's head whipped around to stare at him. "We're grown-ass men," he said with a shrug. "Let's act like it."

Alex wanted to fight, he could see it on the guy's face. That toddler tantrum building up, but to Micah's surprise he took a deep breath and nodded.

Just then Miguel, their bass player came in, devil's horns flying.

"Hey fuckers! Thought you could do this shit without me?" he shouted. He looked thin and pale, his months in the hospital having taken their tool. But he was on his feet with all the energy of the scrawny, mouthy nineteen-year-old kid who'd answered Micah's want ad for a bass player seven years ago and then brought a groove to his music he'd never even imagined.

"Some things never change, huh?" Alex said with a grin and ran off to clasp hands with Miguel.

No. Some things never changed.

But some things had to.

CHAPTER
Twenty~Seven

SUNDAY NIGHT after the big family dinner, Helen was in bed, a rare third glass of wine on the bedside table next to her. Alice had made chicken noodle soup like they were all in need of some comfort, but Helen had been too keyed up to even eat.

Bea caught on to her sort of mid-level hyperness and got revved up, which at least was a distraction. She'd taken all the kids, even the teenagers, outside into the early summer twilight and played a rather epic game of hide and seek.

Now, close to midnight, her heart was still too big in her chest. Every beat felt thick and full and she wanted…God. She wanted everything. She wanted change all at once. She wanted the very next version of herself right now.

She wanted Micah.

Which, she fully understood, was ridiculous.

She'd walked out of that cottage without saying a word. What right did she have to want more? And what *more* could there even be between them?

Helen had finalized all the posters and social media graphics for the picnic. She'd compiled her final list of things that Micah had agreed to and drafted a schedule with pick-up and drop-off times.

On her phone she had the email all written with both Jo and Micah in the address line.

This was business, she was aware. But she still felt flushed. Excited.

"Come on, Helen," she breathed. "Be a grown-up."

She hit Send.

Within minutes there was a reply from Micah. Breathlessly, she opened it.

You drive a hard bargain, Helen. This all looks good to me, I'll see you there.

Right.

She stared at the words, stunned at how easy he made them seem like friends. The underlying intimacy, all while being completely businesslike. *See? Take a page from—*

A text message binged on her phone.

From Micah.

You're awake?

I am, she responded, her heartbeat in her throat. *How are rehearsals?*

Great. Miguel's back. He brings a good energy. How are you?

If she wrote, *I miss you,* what would happen? Anything? Would he shut her down? Maybe that would be a gift, putting an end to this little infatuation.

I miss you, she wrote.

Silence on his end. Not even three dots. Well, she thought, there's the—

Her phone rang. It was Micah, and she was so surprised she accidentally dropped it in her blankets, and then it got lost for a second and by the time she answered it she was sure he'd have hung up.

"Hello?"

"Helen."

Just his voice in her ear changed the chemistry of her whole body. She was a puddle in this single bed. "You left," he said. "Without saying a word."

"I know. It just…seemed easier."

"Was it?"

Nothing about this week had been easy. She'd missed him every step of the way. "No," she said. "I barely know you and I miss you."

"Barely know me?" he laughed. "You know more about me than just about anyone in the world, Helen."

He made it seem so simple. Like the time frame didn't mean anything. Like his rock-star status and her single-mom-living-with-her-parents status didn't mean anything.

"I'm moving out," she said.

"Really? Where are you going?"

"Just an apartment in Catskill but…not until after the picnic. There's just too much going on before that."

"What does Bea think?"

She loved that he asked about her. It was the smallest thing, but she just loved it.

"The complex has a pool, so she's happy."

"Good," he said. "You both deserve to be happy."

"How are things with your brother?"

"We're working on it. Hey," he said. "I have to go, we're about to go back into rehearsal."

"It's midnight!"

"Well, it's not like we start at dawn, you know what I mean? But listen…can I call you again? Tomorrow night?"

"Sure," she said. "Of course."

"It's a date," he said.

The Next Night

"I prefer disco?"

"That is what he said. In, like, the thickest Russian accent I've ever heard. *I prefer disco.*"

"And he's a bodyguard?" she asked. "With a twin brother? And you're okay with it?" She rolled over onto her side in her bed. She'd turned the light off on her bedside table and now was in a quiet, dark cocoon full of his voice.

"Well, the disco is a bit much. But having a body man again is a good thing. My brother and I need help getting over some bad habits. I think this will help."

"That's very grown-up of you," she said. "I can't be around to bail you out of jail all the time."

"Well, that's a shame. Maybe we should do it once more, for old times' sake?"

"You got a strange idea of fun, Micah."

"You loved it. Don't pretend."

She couldn't. She couldn't pretend. Or lie. "I had so much fun," she said.

"So, when you are factoring me in for the picnic, please factor in my new shadow, Ivan."

"His name is Ivan?"

"It's very cold war around here," he laughed. "But he's a nice guy. He was an Olympic wrestler."

"This gets weirder and weirder."

Everything was weird. These phone calls were strange. Her feelings were freaking her out

She was falling in love with him. It was happening and she didn't know how to stop it. She didn't want to stop it.

"Micah," she said. *Why are you calling me? Why are you doing this? Do you feel what I feel? Am I wrong? Am I crazy?*

"Hey, sorry, Helen. I have to go," he said after some noise on his end of the line. "Tomorrow night?"

"Sure."

The Next Night

• • •

"You sent out the press release about the picnic," Micah said.

"We sold out of tickets in ten minutes, Micah," she said. It had been a wild day. She'd sent out the press release and put up all the social media, tagging Band of Outlaws and Micah's Instagram and TikTok accounts, and almost immediately Micah did an Instagram live about the picnic and what Haven House did, and then everything went out of control.

"That's good, right?"

"We're going to need more food. More drinks. More security," she said with a laugh.

"Do you need help with that? Financially?"

"You have done more than enough. You changed the game for us, Micah. I don't know how to thank you."

"You did it, Helen. With all your blackmail. How are all the preparations going?"

They were less than three weeks away at this point, and the truth was that her days were really full. With so much growth, she was trying to anticipate problems she couldn't even imagine. "They're good."

"How about your dirty auction?"

"My bachelors? They're excited. Everyone is. One of the fire fighters is donating driving lessons for teenagers. Billy is donating free oil changes for a year."

"Billy?" he said, his voice sharp and she didn't want to read too much into it, but the guy was radiating some jealous vibes.

"One of the bachelors."

"You're not thinking of getting your oil changed, are you?" he asked. Poor Billy, she thought, everything he volunteered just sounded dirty.

"I just got mine changed," she said, surprised by her own audacity.

"That's right, you did," he said.

She laughed and shifted in the bed, pulling the blankets up around her hips.

"Where are you?" he asked.

"Bed!" she said. "It's midnight."

"You're in your bed right now." His voice dropped and she felt goose bumps ripple over her skin. That blanket was now too hot. "I think I just figured out a way you can thank me."

"Is this the part where you ask me what I'm wearing?"

"What are you wearing?"

She glanced down at her pink tank top and her sleep shorts covered in bright red lips.

Not very sexy.

"Not much," she said and he laughed, groaning in his throat. "Where are you?"

"In the hallway outside the rehearsal space."

"Oh," she said, the goose bumps vanishing. That wasn't very sexy.

"But…" She heard his boots against concrete as he walked. Then there was a door opening and then clicking shut. "Guess where I am now?"

"I have no idea."

"Our closet."

Our closet. Oh God, she really liked this guy. "That might have been one of the most embarrassing moments of my life," she said, trying to push her feeling down into something manageable, but they were like the dogs when called, wild and full of animal love.

"Listen, Helen. I will dig into that with you tomorrow, but right now we've got about ten minutes before I have to get back on stage and I'm thinking about something else."

"What are you thinking about?" she whispered.

"Listening to you come."

And just like that, the picnic was gone and so was his concert rehearsal. The farm. The distance. It was just him and her and this desire that came up out of nowhere. Her body was ready.

She rolled over onto her side, slipping her fingers under the waist of the sleep shorts, over the curve of her belly, down between her legs. Where she was already wet, just listening to his voice over the phone. She'd been wet every night listening to his voice. Trying to go to sleep keyed up and half in...love? Lust? Something.

"Tell me," she whispered. "What would you do if you were here?"

His laugh was pure wickedness. Dirty talking phone sex was a highwire act. Too much thinking and it was ridiculous, but with his voice and the way he made her feel, the words *pussy* and *cock* and *fuck you so good* and *fill you up* were perfect. Beyond perfect. They were a filthy dream come true.

"Are you close?" he asked.

She made a sound in her throat, a gasping purr. Words completely beyond her.

"Come for me, baby," he said, and it was just right. Just perfectly right. And she was coming. Seeing stars, shooting through the universe to his side in that closet. She wished more than anything that he was with her. Or she was there.

"Helen?"

"Hmmm?"

"Can you take a selfie, right now, and send it to me?" he asked.

Oh, that was hot too. She lifted her phone above her head and flipped the camera so she saw herself on the screen. She was flushed and her hair was wild around her head. The strap of her pink cami was down one arm and she looked a little naked and a lot satisfied and, well, beautiful.

She took the picture and sent it.

"Yep," he said after a second. "Exactly how I imagined you."

Micah

Dinner break always took place around midnight. Catering brought in Caesar salad and fries and steak and he thought of the Riverview Inn and that dinner that Alice made.

He had to say something to Helen. At this point, the lie of omission was just a fucking lie. They'd been talking nearly every single night for weeks now. There'd been phone sex and conversation. They'd even watched an episode of some television show she loved while on the phone with each other.

He hadn't said anything, convinced it was something he needed to say in person. But he was falling for her so hard. He wondered if she'd told Jonah and Daphne that they were talking, because Jonah would not like that. But, well, a disapproving father was not the biggest of the obstacles between them.

He glanced down at his phone where he'd turned his screen saver into the picture of Helen after the first time they'd had phone sex. She was ethereal in the glow of that lamp, her post-orgasmic flush making her all rosy. He could stare at this picture all day.

"Hey," Alex said, coming to sit next to him at the table set up in the corner. He had two plates of food. One was just french fries. Neither of them were for Micah. "This picnic thing you're doing two days after Madison Square Garden?"

"Haven House? What about it?"

"You sure it's smart? Two days after Madison Square Garden?"

"I'll be fine," he said. There'd been a time before the lockdown when the band had been hard-drinking and hard-living and it would have been impossible to leave the city and go play a picnic and think he might be sober.

"What's the big fucking deal about this place? Is it just the girl?"

"Again, her name is Helen," Micah said with patience. "And she's in my life, so how about you call her by her name."

Alex sat back, his blue eyes wide. "Wow. Look at you. So, are you doing all this stuff just for the girl? Because I think you're trying—"

"Haven House is a charity for single moms and their kids. They help moms struggling with addiction and living in poverty.

They give the kids a chance to be kids outside of the strain of living in fear or stress."

Alex sat back, very still. Very quiet. A version of his brother he didn't always see.

"How do you know about it?" Alex asked.

"How do you think I know about it?"

They stared at each other, and Micah's old habit was to catalog the differences between them and to get angry about it. But there was so much similarity.

"Mom went there?" Alex asked.

Micah nodded.

"With you." Micah nodded again. "Where was I?"

"You stayed with Peter." Alex nodded, like that made sense, but his jaw was tight. And his hand was in a fist beside the fries, and it was ridiculous but it was their childhood all over again. What Micah had, Alex wanted—even the shitty things.

"I used to be really jealous of the way you two had this whole bond without me. This, like, secret language I would never understand."

"I'm sorry if we made you feel that way. But it wasn't…good, Alex. It was scary. And Mom changed everything to protect you, you know. To give you a better childhood."

Alex nodded, biting his bottom lip. "Dad used to feel the same way, you know? Jealous. I think that's why he was so hard on you."

As insight it was more than a little stunning coming from Alex. All Micah could do was nod. This was unfamiliar territory for them and he had to think it was good. Progress.

"You want some fries?" Alex asked, pushing the plate over to him.

Micah's phone buzzed and he knew without looking that it was Helen. "Sorry," he said, unable to hide his smile. "I gotta take this."

Alex nodded. "Hey," he said as Micah was walking away. "It's really good to see you happy. You deserve it."

The words threw him for a loop and he was rattled when he answered the call and heard Helen's voice.

"Hey," she said. "Did you get a chance—"

"Helen, I want you to come to the Madison Square Garden show."

"Oh…okay. Sure."

"And I need to tell you something. Something important but I don't want to do it over the phone. I'll send a car for everyone and after the show we'll get a chance to talk. Really talk."

"Micah," she said, and he could hear the smile in her voice. "I'd love to. I'll be there."

CHAPTER
Twenty-Eight

Helen

All the details for the picnic were taken care of. Going to New York City for the night was maybe a little stressful, but she was not about to say no. Bea was staying with Daniella and her daughter and going swimming in the morning at the apartment complex pool.

Josie was in town for the picnic, and she insisted they go shopping in Catskill for new clothes for the night. A sparkly shirt. Brand new jeans. A little fake leather jacket that was kind of like wearing a ziplock bag. And booties with a sexy zipper and sharp heels.

Josie curled Helen's blond hair and loaned her a bright red lippie.

"You're smoking hot," Josie said, looking over her shoulder in the mirror.

Helen couldn't even argue. The woman looking back at her was young and alive in a way she hadn't felt...ever.

Micah sent a car, which Jonah wanted to decline.

"It's really unnecessary, isn't it?" he asked, even as they were waiting for the car to arrive. "We can take the train and walk."

"Look at my shoes, Jonah," she said.

He glanced down and winced. "I guess the car makes sense."

They stood, each of them looking out a different window for a sign of the car. "He had coffee delivered," she said, tilting her head to see down the road past the driveway. "At that hotel we stayed at. He had coffee and toiletries delivered, and I'm telling you it seemed like the most decadent thing I'd ever seen. He bought me underwear." She laughed. "Like, a Walmart three pack."

Her parents were silent and she turned to find them staring at her. "What?"

"You really like him," Mom said.

"I do, Mom. I really like him." It felt good to say it out loud. They'd been talking every night on the phone for a month. This was past a rock star infatuation; she *liked* him. As a person. Admired him. Desired him.

She was recklessly falling in love with him.

Mom and Jonah shared a worried look.

"What's that look for?" she asked. "I thought you'd be excited. Me moving on and everything. You've been trying to get me to date someone for months."

"Has he talked to you about the new songs?"

"No," she said, wondering why they cared. "What does that have to do with anything? I don't like him just because of his music."

"Have you listened to the new album?" Jonah asked. "Really listened to it?"

"Why?" The truth was, she still hadn't devoted a whole lot of energy to listening to that album. She'd been busy and there was something about the tone of the new songs that made her feel... too much. It was like a raw nerve. And she understood that people were loving the album for exactly that reason, but it hit a little too close to home right now.

"Just...you should listen to it," Jonah said.

"Well, I will tonight, won't I?" she said. "Now stop being weird—we're going to go have a great time."

The tickets were there for them at Will Call. Front row VIP with backstage passes.

"Oh my god," she said, holding up the lanyards. And whatever Jonah and Mom's weird mood back at the house had been about, they were both caught up in the thrill of being in the city and out at the concert.

Mom had a hotdog and a soft pretzel from a vendor on the sidewalk.

"Look at you," Jonah said, kissing ketchup off Mom's lips. "Being so wild."

They walked into the arena and showed their tickets to the first usher they saw. "Nice," the guy said and directed them to the next usher who stood at the entrance to the floor. "He'll tell you where to go."

That usher directed them to the next usher who stood right at the edge of the stage.

"Where the hell are these seats?" Jonah asked.

There was a tiny section separated from the rest of the floor, right in front of the stage. "Front row VIP," the usher said and moved the partition for them to slide in.

"Don't do that," the usher said as Mom reached out to touch the stage.

The stage was dark, the silhouettes of all the instruments and microphones dramatic against the backdrop. The PA system was playing a Chris Stapleton song and Jonah got three cans of beer from a guy walking around with a cooler strapped to his back.

"To getting back to life," she said, holding up her can for a cheers. "And to you guys, for getting me through the last three years."

Mom's eyes predictably flooded with tears. "We love you, honey."

"And remember," Jonah said. "We're always here when you need us."

Now her eyes were full of tears.

The lights changed and Chris Stapleton was gone and the crowd started to roar. Helen turned to the stage just as all the guys came out. The drummer, Sean, sat at his kit and lifted his drumsticks in the air and the crowd went crazy. Miguel, the bass player, came out shirtless, and there was even more screaming. Then it was Alex, in blue jeans and a black tee-shirt, a guitar across his back like a rock and roll gunslinger.

And then it was Micah. Black jeans and a denim shirt with the sleeves rolled up like he was a man who was about to get some work done.

And she was screaming. Like the thousands of other people in the arena with her, she lost her damn mind and just started screaming.

That's my boyfriend!

"Hey," Micah said into the microphone. "We're Band of Outlaws."

And the music started.

They roared into their biggest hits and the crowd was on their feet dancing. Alex sang "Saturday Morning Pancakes" and she had new painful and real insight into the lyrics.

We got a trailer and a beat-up car. A stack of bills and Saturday morning pancakes. You're my mama and I'm your boy.

She felt Miguel's bass in her chest and Micah's voice in her heartbeat. She looked around at thousands of people watching Micah with nothing less than hero worship in their eyes. He was singing to each and every one of them and they adored him for what he was making them feel.

And he's mine.

It was shamefully empowering. Micah brought thousands of people to their knees.

And she brought him to his knees.

Watching him and wanting him and knowing he wanted her, too, it felt like trying to catch lightning in her hands.

The song finished and the band rolled right into another song. Micah stepped up to the microphone with his head tilted their way and she saw the moment he saw them. His whole face transformed.

"There's my girl," he said, and she would have fallen right on her face if she wasn't sandwiched up with dancing strangers.

He winked at her and she lifted her hand in a wave.

"Folks we've got some special guests," he said into the microphone, looking out at the screaming people. "The fine people at Haven House are here! Go check out the good work they've done. We're real glad they're here. We're real glad all of you are here. It's been too damn long."

The band came in hard and the crowd cheered and fist bumped and danced in the aisles. Micah stepped away from the microphone and back toward the wings. The band watched him as he did it. Alex lifted a finger and twirled it in the air and the band kept improvising until Micah was back on stage, singing his soul out into the microphone.

Suddenly there was a giant mountain of a man standing in the security area between the VIP area and the stage. Helen, Jonah and Daphne all turned to look at him. He was the kind of size you could not ignore.

"Ivan?" Helen asked, taking a stab in the dark. The big man with cauliflower ears and a shaved bald head grinned.

"Yes!" he said. "Micah wants me to bring you all backstage," he said. "Climb under the barricade. Is all right."

Helen looked back at her parents who were shaking their heads. "You go," Jonah said. "We'll stay here."

"You sure? There's probably an after—"

"I'll come get them for the after party," Ivan offered, and she agreed and she was suddenly being whisked past security and through heavy double doors down cement hallways where

Micah's voice sounded muffled but the drums sounded like they were right in her ears.

She recognized people. Famous people. Or people who looked like they should be famous, and Ivan led her right past them and they watched her go like she was the interesting one.

Oh, she thought with an internal giggle. *This really is wild.*

And suddenly they were standing among all the roadies in black pants and shirts. Women with headsets and iPads, who looked like they were in charge of a space mission. They walked around a cement half wall and then there she was. Back stage.

Five feet away Band Of Outlaws was bathed in spotlights as they played their guts out, giving everyone in that stadium some much-needed catharsis. Micah pulled the microphone from the stand and walked over to his brother, threw his arm around his shoulders and the two of them, grinning, sang together into the microphone.

She danced and sang and lost herself to the music. She lost herself to Micah. To what he made her feel. And far too soon it was over. The band went to stand at the edge of the stage, bowing. Holding hands and lifting them into the lights and screams of their fans.

And then they turned and ran backstage.

Sean came by, dripping sweat. Miguel ran over to a woman who had, no kidding, an oxygen tank waiting for him. Alex walked by with a quick wink to grab a beer and a towel. And then it was Micah.

Micah with his eyes on fire. His shirt soaked through. His hair sticking to his face in clumps. He'd come to work and he'd done it.

I want to fuck him.

The whole place wanted to fuck him but she was going to. And he was looking at her like he felt the same way. Everyone backstage vanished. And it was his blue eyes and nothing else.

"Five minutes to encore," one of the women with headphones in charge of shit said. "Five minutes."

Micah stopped right in front of her, smelling of sweat and sex and rock and roll. And instead of saying anything he just grabbed her hand, pulling her behind him, walking so fast she had to run in her sexy heeled booties.

"Micah!" she cried, laughing as he ignored people wanting to give him bottles of water and slap his hand. He shoved open a small door that was nestled into wall surrounded by coiled cables and ropes. He yanked her in after him and the door shut behind them. It was a tiny bathroom.

"What are we—" she asked, but then he kissed her. No, scratch that. He inhaled her. Mauled her. It was primal and raw and she was with him in a heartbeat. He grabbed at her breasts. Her ass. Shoved her up onto a small sink so he could get between her legs, grinding his cock against her.

Yep. Yes. More. All of that and more.

She had five minutes. Less than five minutes to gorge herself on rock star and she went right for his belt. Yanking leather and damp denim out of the way until she got to his underwear. Also soaked and she fucking loved it. She was bathed in his sweat, her face raw from his beard.

"Fuck. Helen." He growled against her throat, opening up her belt, unzipping her jeans. And then looking her deep in the eyes, he lifted his hand, spit on his fingers and slid them between her legs.

It was the most rock-and-roll thing she'd seen all night. And there'd been a lot of rock and roll.

"Fuck me," she said, her hand around his cock, his fingers between her legs

"No condom." He pressed his head against hers, his fingers making easy work of her.

"I'm on the pill."

"I'm clean."

He yanked her off the sink, turned her and she bent over the sink, kicking her legs out as wide as she could with the denim around her knees.

Without warning he was deep inside of her with a thrust she felt in the back of her throat. She had to brace herself against the mirror, her hands spread wide. She felt his fingertips digging into her hips so hard she'd have bruises. Her hair flopped over her face and she was making an animal noise in back of her throat. The orgasm came after her with teeth and nails, and it was going to be the kind of pleasure that hurt and she had never experienced it before.

It was the kind of pleasure in Micah's songs and now it was hers.

She looked up and caught his face in the mirror. The way he was watching her, like she was the only thing in this world that mattered, and she was spellbound.

Helpless.

She broke into a million pieces right in front of his eyes. His fingers between her legs. She was lost and found and lost again, and it was the fucking best.

He yanked her up by her shoulder, finding some leverage that he liked and pounded into her while she watched it all in the mirror. Who was that couple? That felt so much? That looked so good?

Us.

"I love you," she said. His eyes flew to hers for one breathless second. Like jumping off a cliff, and then the orgasm had him in its teeth, too. And he wrapped his arms around her chest, heaving himself into her.

"Fuck," he said. Again and again. *Fuck* and *Helen*. And *I can't stop.*

And then it was over. And they were breathing hard in a tiny bathroom backstage in Madison Square Garden.

And she'd told him she loved him.

And he wasn't looking her in the eye anymore.

"Are you okay?" he asked, carefully stepping away from her. She felt the ooze of his come between her legs and grabbed toilet paper to try and clean herself up.

"Fine," she said with a smile. "Really…good."

"That was…" He blew out a breath, pushing his hair back. "Intense."

"I'm sorry. What I said…"

"It's okay." His fake heartbreaker grin made an appearance. "It happens. We got carried away."

She stilled. Carried away? Is that what he thought? A month of nightly phone calls? Everything they'd shared. Embarrassment rolled through her in a prickly hot wave. How had she been so wrong?

She pulled up her pants and did up the belt, and he put his fingers on her chin, lifting her face to see him. "I need to tell you something," he said. "It's about the new album."

The new album? Jesus, was it so important she listen to the damn thing?

There was a pounding on the door.

"Micah!" Alex shouted. "Ten thousand people are screaming our names. We gotta go."

"You need to go," she said, patting his shoulder. "We'll talk later."

Micah threw open the door and was gone. Whisked out of the darkness of backstage back into the blinding spotlight and she did a walk of shame backstage in Madison Square Garden. It was crowded now. All those people in the halls had made it into the wings and were taking selfies and singing along, and she felt too raw to stand there with strangers.

She found Ivan standing near the door, his arms over his chest, looking terrifying. But also kind of endearing. She was glad he was around to keep Micah safe.

"Can you take me back to my parents?" she shouted and he nodded and led her back through the concrete hallways through the big doors into the sweaty screaming darkness filled with thousands of Band of Outlaws fans.

She was sore between her legs. And a little in her heart. That would get worse, she knew it. There was heartbreak coming but it wasn't here yet.

"Hey!" Mom said when Helen ducked up under the barricade to stand next to them again. "You okay?" she shouted.

"Fine!" she shouted back and hoped her parents couldn't smell sex on her.

"This is a new song off the album. It's my favorite song." Micah looked out at the crowd.

He was inside me, she thought. *I told him I loved him and he asked me if I was all right and I think I might have made a fool of myself.*

But she clung to the idea that he wanted to talk to her. Maybe he didn't love her, right now. But maybe he might?

Micah turned his face and found her there with her parents like he knew that after what happened she'd need to be around familiar people. His face was an open wound. Ravaged. And all she could think was that he didn't love her back and it hurt him so much "This is for the bravest woman I've ever met. Helen," he said and broke into "This is Forgiveness."

She flinched from the song; there really was something about it she did not like. "Hey," she said turning to her parents. "You want to—"

"Listen," Jonah said. "Listen to the words."

"I don't…" She shook her head. The roar of the crowd and everything made it hard. Or made it easy to be hard. "I can't…"

"Honey," Mom yelled. And something in her face was deeply scary. She reached out and held Helen's hand. Micah hit the chorus.

Hurting you won't change a thing. Hurting you won't ease my pain.

She sucked in a breath that didn't come. There was no air.

That was…familiar. But why? Because she'd heard it a bunch. The song was all over the radio. But she hadn't. Really. Every time it came on she turned it off. She'd heard it once at the rehearsal space and it had sent her into a panic attack.

The only way forward for any of us is forgiveness.

It was from her victim statement.

"But he wouldn't..." use those words in a song. Would he? Take all her pain and make a song?

Jonah nodded.

Oh God. She folded over at the waist.

And all at once those songs she didn't like listening to—"Forgiveness." "White-knuckled." "Ghosts." It was because they were full of her words. Her pain.

Jonah's hand was around her waist holding her up.

All those songs he was writing while they were together on that road trip. *Relentless.* Was he...just using her? Was any of it real or was it all for his music?

Well, she knew the answer to that, didn't she? It was in his silence after she said I love you.

Mom's arms came around her and she looked out at the crowd of people singing her words. Their pain and her pain. And the guy on stage using all of it for his own purpose.

"Get me out of here," she said.

CHAPTER
Twenty~Nine

MICAH

She was there, her face pale and stricken, every word he was singing doing her some kind of harm, and he wished he could stop, but even if he stopped singing, the thousands of people in the arena would keep going.

The words Helen had said to the woman who killed her fiancé had become the words he used in a song, had become the words thousands of people had internalized and were screaming back at him.

It had a life of its own, which was what good songs did. Songs that touched something visceral.

She just didn't know. He'd put her in this position without her knowledge or consent.

When he couldn't bear witness to her pain anymore, he turned to the other side of the stage, lifting his finger and pointing up to the nosebleed section so they could roar their approval.

When he turned back to look for her…she was gone.

The band finished. Gathered at the edge of the stage for one last bow. He felt his brother's arm over his shoulders.

"We did it, Micah!" Alex shouted in his ear. And it was true, everything about the night had been an astronomical success. The kind of night he'd never dreamed was possible as a kid living in that shitty trailer, wondering if they could pay for heat or water that month.

And it felt like ash in his mouth.

"We're the motherfucking Band of Outlaws!" Miguel shouted and they all threw guitar picks and drumsticks into the chanting crowd and he ran off stage.

"Great show!" Jo said with a rare smile. It must have been good if she was happy.

"I need my phone," he said. Not even engaging with her excitement. All around him were people trying to get his attention. Slapping his back and sticking cameras in his face.

"Micah," Jo said, leaning forward. "You have two interviews tonight. *Rolling Stone* and *The Times*. You can't...leave." She looked at him like she knew what he was thinking. That he was going to get in a car and go find her.

"I'll do the interviews. Just give me the phone."

She handed him his phone and he took off down one of the hallways until he got someplace kind of quiet. He dialed Helen's number. It rang and then went to voicemail. He called again. Same thing. One more time and it was finally picked up.

"Helen," he said. "I've been trying to tell—"

"Micah. It's Jonah. Stop calling. She is in no shape to talk to you."

He closed his eyes, his chest tearing open.

Fuck. He could do the interviews and then get out to Athens... he looked at his watch.

"And," Jonah said. "If you have any respect for her, or her daughter, you won't show up at the farm tonight."

"I'm sorry," he said. "Tell her I'm sorry. Can you do that?"

"I will," Jonah said and hung up.

Thirty

THE DAY of the picnic dawned like a picture. Bright yellow sun, clear blue sky. Warm temperatures, cool breeze. It was a day made for picnics. And she'd been so prepared, so completely on top of everything, that it felt like all she really had to do was stand around with a clipboard in her hand.

The stage was being built.

Bouncy castles were being blown up.

Face painting. Sack races. The silent auction. The food tent. Tables and chairs.

All of it being handled.

"It looks like they don't need you," Josie said, looping her arm through Helen's. Helen didn't even respond. She felt numb inside, like she'd been cleaned out. "Oh, Helen," Josie said, and her cousin/best friend pulled her into her arms. Helen rested her head on Josie's shoulder, the beautiful auburn hair tickling her nose, and she didn't even care.

"This isn't a broken heart," she told Josie.

"Are you sure?"

"My heart's been broken before and it didn't feel like this." She hadn't been numb when Evan died. She'd been a rage of pain. She stepped back and squared her shoulders. "This feels like embarrassment. That's all."

"Okay," Josie said, like she didn't believe her even a little bit. "What can I do to help?"

Helen looked around at all the work being done and she didn't have an answer. "Stand here with me so I don't look stupid?" she asked with a laugh.

"No problem." Josie slung her arm back through Helen's just as a black town car pulled into the parking area and slowed to a stop right outside the gates they'd set up to control the crowd they were expecting.

Micah jumped out of the back seat. But then so did Alex. Out of the front seat came Ivan. They all slammed the doors and whoever was driving followed the instructions of the police officer who was controlling the comings and goings of trucks and cars.

Micah wore a grey tee-shirt and all his jewelry. The necklaces and bracelets. The ring on his thumb. He had a black bandana sticking out of the back pocket of his jeans, which were rolled just right over his beat-up boots.

"Holy shit," Josie said. "He is smoking hot."

"Not helpful, Josie!"

"I know, I know, I'm sorry, but oh my god."

"Yeah, he kind of takes your breath away," Helen whispered. And your sense. And a little bit of your self-respect. And all of your reason. "I need to go get him set up."

"Nope," Josie said. "That's what I'm doing for you. I'm handling him today."

What a relief it would be. The same way it had been a relief for Jonah to talk to him on the phone the other night on the way home from the concert. But she couldn't hide from him the way she'd been hiding on this mountaintop for the last three years.

She had to face him at some point, and here, surrounded by all the hard work she'd done and the people who loved her, was as good a place as any.

"I got it," Helen said and kissed her cousin's cheek.

She started across the park toward where Micah and Alex had gotten stopped by some fans. They were signing autographs when Micah looked up and saw her. He said something to the person he was talking to, gave Alex a quick glance and started over to her.

He was all long legs and rock-star swagger and it made her breath catch in her throat.

Get it together, Helen.

"Hi," she said, when he was close, grateful for her sunglasses.

"Hi," he said. "Are you all right?"

It was the way he looked at her, like there weren't dozens of people around them. Like she was the only thing that mattered, and it was the exact same look he'd been able to give to thousands of people the other night through a jumbotron. It was part of his gift.

I'm not special.

"I'm fine," she said with a big smile. "Great, actually. As you can see we're off to an amazing start and—"

He reached forward and pulled her glasses from her eyes. "It's me, Helen. I'm not a stranger. Please, don't talk to me like I am."

"I don't know who you are," she said and pulled the glasses away from him so she could put them back on. "You used me," she whispered, the truth of her pain bubbling up from all the places she tried to shove it.

"Holy shit, Micah Sullivan!" one of the volunteers said as he walked by with rolls of raffle tickets. "I heard you were going to be here."

"Hey," Micah said, shaking the guy's hand, taking a quick picture, and the guy moved on. But they were gathering attention.

"Is there someplace we can go and we can talk?" he asked. "Please?"

She nodded and led him over to the area behind the stage where there weren't any people. There was a narrow tract of grass just before the tree line and it was quiet.

"I'm sorry I didn't tell you," he said. "I wanted to. But it just… it just kept being the thing that if I told you it would change everything and I liked the way things were."

"Because you were using me," she said.

"I was inspired by you. Trust me," he sighed. "Trust me, I know it sounds like bullshit but I'm inspired by you constantly, by your bravery—"

"I'm more than the shitty thing that happened to me, Micah."

He stepped closer. "I'm inspired by the way you touch me. And kiss me. The way you feel and taste."

"I'm more than that, too," she snapped, proud of herself for being firm in front of that little onslaught. He grinned, like he knew it. "I just don't know what was real!" she snapped, and for the first time he looked stricken.

"Everything was real, Helen. Every minute. Every thought and touch…"

"Then walk me through it," she said. "You read the article, absolutely plagiarized my words."

"I'm so sorry."

"Oh, trust me, you'll be paying Haven House for the privilege of taking those words." His lip quirked but she scowled, unwilling to be charmed, and he stopped grinning.

"At the beginning of lockdown," he said, "I know I wasn't special and that a lot of people had it worse, but I was struggling. I was alone and isolated and my demons were right there, constantly. And I had stopped drinking, but I had some beer delivered and I put it on my counter and just looked at it, waiting for the minute I would break. And then I read that article in the *New York Times* and it was you—the same girl who sat next to me when I was so scared, and it was like you'd come to me when I needed you most. Twice. It felt like fucking fate, Helen.

"I got rid of the beer and I wrote the songs, inspired by what you'd done and yes, what you'd said. The whole time remembering what you'd done for me when I was a kid. And at first they were just words. You've seen me, I just write shit down. Half of it is nothing. But then I met Danny and he could turn nothing into something amazing, and when he was done with them I had songs. Great songs. Like, the best songs I'd ever written. Songs inspired by you. And I felt…guilty, yeah. But also so fucking lucky that you walked into my life, and then we had that moment in the closet and I knew. Helen, I knew if I let you walk out of my life, I'd be a fucking fool. And I didn't tell you because I wanted *you* to tell me. I wanted you to trust me. I wanted you to stay."

She didn't know how to process any of this. Partly because she wanted so badly for everything to be true.

"I have to go," she whispered.

"I understand," he said. "But I want you to know, all the money I make from the record sales is going into a trust fund for Bea."

She looked up at him, shocked.

"I know she's got a lot of love. And people. And you would never leave her unless…God forbid."

"Don't even say that."

"But we both know shit happens. And love and people are great. But money doesn't hurt."

"How much…" She shook her head. It didn't matter. Money was the least of all these things.

"Currently eight hundred thousand dollars."

"Oh my god," she breathed.

He shrugged like it was ordering coffee to be delivered. Like it was writing a great song on a napkin, like it was all just part of life. And for a moment, bright and hot, she loved him so much. So hard.

"You told me you loved me Helen, and I have loved you for so long."

CHAPTER
Thirty~One

SHE STEPPED BACK, got poked by a pine tree and then, without another word, turned and walked away. *Do I believe this?* she wondered. *How do I believe this?*

As fast as she could, she walked away from that place, her head down, her whole body working on staying upright. The first person she ran into was Jonah.

"Honey," he breathed, and she shook her head and shrugged and shook her head again and tried not to cry. "I saw him arrive. Are you all right?"

"I don't know what to believe," she whispered.

"Tell me."

"He says he loves me."

"I believe that." She looked up at him, wide-eyed and slightly betrayed. "You do?

"I do." He smiled but it was a little sad. "I have been pretty sure he loved you since I saw his face at the farm that night he came to visit. But love without honesty is a trap, Helen."

"He told me the truth. About the songs and how it all happened."

"Do you believe him?"

"I do."

"Do you believe he's tried to redeem himself for what happened?"

"He's taking all the money he's making from sales of the album and putting it in a trust for Bea," she whispered. His eyes went wide.

"Oh." He wrapped his arms around her. "That's really something."

"He tried to tell me," she said. "So many times. That counts for something, doesn't it?"

"Only you can answer that, honey."

The truth was, that wasn't even what was really bothering her. How did she know this was real? That was what she was scared of. "What if I am interesting right now because of the songs and the way I was making him feel and it all goes away?"

"Sure," Jonah said. "That's the risk, with love. But what if it doesn't go away? What if it gets better and you build something amazing? And that's the reward?"

The picnic, without a doubt, was a huge success. And more than that, it was a well-run and orderly success. No surprises. No drama. Lines ran smoothly. The raffle items were going for double and triple the prices listed. The guitar signed by Band of Outlaws was going for more than five grand, and when she walked into the pavilion where all the items were laid out she was surprised to see Alex walking around, schmoozing and shaking hands. Accidentally she met his gaze and she made a super awkward effort to pretend she hadn't. She turned away only to find Bea with Micah in the crowd. Like he was a magnet and she could only look at him. He was sitting on one of the plastic little kid chairs and Bea was reaching up, her tongue between her teeth as she carefully painted a gigantic butterfly on Micah's face.

Oh my god.

Her insides quaked and she clutched her clipboard to her chest to keep herself from…she didn't know. Hurling herself across the park and into his arms.

"Hey."

She turned to find Alex standing beside her.

"Hi," she said, her voice pitched somewhere only dogs could hear.

"Quite a picnic."

"Glad you like it."

"I never knew Micah and Mom came to Haven House when he was young."

"He was keeping that a secret?" she asked. "Wow, the guy likes his secrets."

"They are not secrets," Alex said, jumping to his brother's defense. Which was strange for the guy who left him to fight his fights. "I used to think they were, but recently I've been thinking something else."

She turned, giving him her undivided attention.

"He's written twenty songs about our mom," he said. "And everyone thinks they're good old mama-boy songs but no one ever hears how angry they are. I never heard how angry they are." He gave her his best heartbreaker grin and it was good. Really good. But she'd had some practice lately looking behind rock-star personas and she saw something else there. Something dark behind the devil-may-care face he gave the world. Something sad and a little bit sorry.

"He processes everything by writing about it. If he doesn't write about it, it sits in his stomach for years and he pretends it didn't happen and, yeah, he keeps it a secret. But they're the kind of secrets that hurt him more than anyone else. Unless he writes about them." He shrugged. "If the money he's willing to give you doesn't sway you, maybe that will."

"Sway me toward what?"

"A second chance," he said. "My brother would really like a second chance."

"Mom!" Bea shouted from the face-painting tent. "Look at Micah!"

Micah turned to face Helen and Alex, and they both gasped. A lopsided pink butterfly took up the whole of his face. The wings on his cheeks. The body his broken nose. There was a lot of glitter.

"Good god," Alex laughed. "It must be love."

CHAPTER

Thirty~Two

THE BACHELOR AUCTION was starting up and Josie was the MC. She had a little PA system and a lectern for her notes.

"Let's hear it for the bachelor auction, ladies and gentlemen. The Athens Fire Department has pulled out all the stops this year, so let's bid high and let's bid often. Get your oil changed and support a good cause."

The sun was setting, and the food tents were running out of food and all day people had been coming up to her with their lockboxes full of cash, terrified of how much money was in them. They'd started emptying the lockboxes into a gym bag that she had in the trunk of her car. And Jonah had taken the gym bag to the safe at Haven House. Twice.

Helen sat down in one of the chairs set up in front of the stage, to rest her feet and enjoy Josie and the bachelor auction. Mom and Bea stopped by, and Bea crawled up into her lap. Mom sat down beside her.

"Excuse me," Alice muttered, squeezing past them to sit on the far side of Jonah. "God, my feet are killing me. Do any of these fire fighters give foot rubs?"

"No one is touching your feet but me," Gabe said, leaning up from the empty seat behind his wife to kiss her neck. "Oh wow, you smell delicious."

"Pulled pork. Which, for the record, was a total hit."

Delia and Max sat down too.

Jonah walked by, and Alice moved over so he could sit next to Mom.

"Hey," she said, kissing his cheek. "How is the money-running operation?"

"Do you want to know how much we've made so far?" he asked, eyebrows wiggling.

"One hundred thousand dollars," Alice said, and Jonah turned wide eyes on her. "How did you guess?"

"I ran a restaurant for years—you get a feel for how much cash is going over the bar."

"Are you serious?" Helen asked. Last year they'd made fifteen grand and called it a gigantic success.

Jonah nodded. "It's because of Micah," he said.

And she knew that.

"Hey, everyone in the audience, we have a treat for you," Josie said and looked right out and winked at Helen. "A very special bachelor is here and he's donating..." She looked behind her to someone off the side of the stage that was hidden by some of the crowd milling about. She put her hand over the mic but the crowd could still hear her say "What are you donating?"

She nodded and turned back to the mic.

"A private concert. Five songs. Your choice. Ladies and gentleman the last bachelor of the night—Micah Sullivan."

Micah jumped up on the stage, arms in the air, still wearing Bea's face paint.

Every time she'd seen him over the course of the last five hours, he'd been engaged. Signing autographs, shaking hands, at one point working a food station. The whole time with a glittery pink butterfly on his face. It was going to be all over social media.

She looked over at her family who were all staring at her.

What if you build something amazing and that's the reward?

I love him. I love him and he loves me. And I have to just have faith that it's enough. It felt in this moment surrounded by people she loved and something she'd built with her own hands, like more than enough. Like she couldn't hold onto everything she felt. It was more than she'd ever felt in her life. More than she'd dreamt was possible to feel.

"We're going to start the bidding with…" Josie looked a little lost. "I don't know, a thousand dollars?"

It went fast. A thousand. Two. Five.

If she was going to make a move she needed to do it fast.

"Do you want to bid?" she asked her daughter.

"Yes!" She clapped.

"When I stand up, say ten thousand dollars. But you have to say it really loud."

Bea nodded and Helen got to her feet.

"Ten thousand dollars," Bea screamed and Helen's ears rang.

On stage Micah turned, his eyes finding them in the crowd. And what she saw there was worth every risk. Of course, she would give him a second chance, because he was giving her one as well.

She smiled at him, the whole of her heart in her eyes.

He smiled back with the whole of his heart, too.

"Sold!" he shouted, and the crowd, realizing what was happening, started clapping.

"Go, Helen," Mom said, pushing her butt. "Go up there."

This was a little more public than she liked, but Micah was a public guy. And she was standing with her family at her back and the man she loved in front of her. Still carrying Bea she started walking up along the edge of the chairs, the crowd parting to let her through until finally she was on the edge of the stage.

Micah smiled down at her and lifted Bea up onto the stage and then held a hand out for Helen. It was only a foot off the ground, but she took his hand and was pulled up onto the stage and immediately into his arms.

"Thank you," he said.

She leaned back, the tears she'd been blinking back rolling down her face. "Thank you."

"For what?" he said with a butterfly her daughter had painted on his face.

"For taking my pain and turning it into something beautiful," she said. And then she kissed him. She didn't care about the crowd or her family watching. She didn't even care about the face paint that was now going to be all over her.

She just cared about him.

"All right lovebirds," Josie said. "As much as I love watching my cousin make out with a rock star, I believe we were promised a concert!"

The crowd cheered and Micah finally pulled away.

"To be continued," Micah said to her.

Alex was walking out on stage with two guitars while Cameron, who'd been volunteering with the tech staff, brought out two microphones on stands. He gave Bea a high five and Helen got a one-armed hug as they both scurried out of the way.

"Hey," Micah said into the microphone as he put the guitar strap over his head. "My brother Alex is here to help out. I hope you don't mind?"

The crowd cheered its approval and Alex lifted his hand.

"But before we sing for you, I feel like my brother is missing something." Micah grinned at Alex, who started shaking his head.

"No, man, come on," Alex said.

"Bea?" Micah asked, looking back for her. "Do you think he's missing something?"

"A butterfly!" she yelled.

"Yeah, I think so too," Micah said with total seriousness. "Can we get some face paint and a chair up here? And I'll sing while Bea here works her magic."

The crowd was loving this, and Helen could only stand there with her hands pressed to her lips as Cameron came out with a chair. Alex sat down in it and Bea got to work painting his face.

"Now," Micah said, "do we have any requests?"

"'Forgiveness,'" Helen yelled, and he turned to face her. "Play 'Forgiveness.'"

"Anything for you," he said and started into the first notes of the song. The crowd, her family a part of it, started clapping, keeping the beat.

This is the reward.

I gotta tell him about that, she thought. *I bet there's a song in there.*

Epilogue

ONE YEAR Later

First stop was the farm. He knocked on the screen door and Daphne, drying her hands on a dish towel, came over to open it. "Micah," she said sternly. "You have to stop knocking. You can come in."

"Not after the last time," he said with a wink, and Daphne blushed. When he and Helen arrived at the farm three days ago, they'd walked in and caught Daphne and Jonah kissing. Like… kissing with *intent*. "Who knows what I'll walk into?"

Daphne rolled her eyes at him and he walked into the cozy warmth of the Athens Organics kitchen.

The tour was over as of the previous week, and it had been hectic but also extremely amazing. Sold out shows across North America. Bea and Helen had joined them for the European leg and it had been a real family affair with Miguel bringing his wife. Jonah and Helen came to two shows and then rented a car and drove through Italy. They took Bea with them and Helen traveled with the band. Danny made the trip for a few shows. He and Alex made up, which warmed Micah's heart, and Danny came out for a few songs to play the harmonica. It was absolutely fantastic and Alex made a strong case for Danny joining them for the rest of the tour—and to Micah's shock and Jo's logistical frustration, Danny agreed.

All in all, it was a totally different vibe than their last tour through Europe. Though Alex kept their rock street cred alive by punching a Nazi skinhead in Paris. And Micah and Helen had created a very strange but completely satisfying tradition of having sex in backstage bathrooms in arenas all over Europe.

But during that week while Bea was with Daphne and Jonah, something had happened. Something big. And he and Helen were still trying to figure it out. And there were a lot of moving parts, but one thing he knew for sure.

She had to make an honest man out of him.

"How are you guys settling in over there?" she asked. They'd been put in Cabin Nine.

"Helen's still upside down with jetlag," he said. Which was true but also a lie. "Is Jonah here?"

"Yeah. I think he's in the office, go on back."

"Actually, I'd like to talk to the two of you. You wanna…?" he tilted his head towards the door that led to the rest of the house.

Daphne had not been born yesterday and her eyes went wide and filled with tears.

"Just…" He laughed. "Let me do this before you start crying."

"Of course," she said and led him through the dining room and the living room into the small office that she and Jonah shared. It was a big sprawling house full of mismatched furniture and too much junk that they never around to throwing away and so many memories the place nearly glowed.

It was exactly the kind of house he wanted for his family.

My family.

His throat was suddenly thick with emotion.

"Hey, honey," Daphne said, stepping into the office. Jonah

looked up as Daphne crossed the room to kiss his head and then sit on the arm of his chair. "Micah has something he wants to talk about."

"Yeah?" Jonah asked, his face open. He and Jonah had gone through a journey together, complicated, maybe, by the fact that Jonah really was a fan of his music. But as a man, Micah had to win him over and he liked to think he had. Not by flying them around the world to see concerts. But by steadily and truly loving Helen with all of his heart. "What's up?"

"I would like your permission to marry your daughter," he said to both of them. "I think you know how I feel about her. And I think you can be confident that I will take care of her."

Jonah and Daphne shared a long look. Really long. Too long? Micah suddenly got nervous.

"If you're worried about the life-"

"We aren't worried about anything. We know you love her, son," Jonah said, and Micah, to his great embarrassment, felt tears burn in his eyes. Son. No one had called him that since his mother. "We're just really happy you came along to give her a second chance."

"You absolutely have our blessing," Daphne said. "Do you have a ring?"

"Daphne?" Jonah said. "Of course he has a ring."

He did not have a ring. He didn't think a ring was all that important. Helen was not a woman who needed diamonds.

Shit. Was she?

"It's been...well, it's been busy." Daphne was shaking her head in total disappointment. "I don't know—I thought she'd want to pick something out."

"Lame," Daphne said.

Jonah scooched his wife off the arm of his chair and got to his feet. He opened the safe under the desk and took out a black velvet box.

"Oh, Jonah," Daphne sighed.

"This was my mother's ring," Jonah said. "It is not fancy. Patrick could not afford fancy. But she wore it every day of her life. And I've been waiting for a chance to pass it on to someone. I want you to understand you can replace it with something flashier, but you can't propose empty-handed, son. You just can't."

He handed the black velvet box to Micah, who carefully opened it.

It wasn't fancy. But it was perfect. A small diamond in a simple setting.

"Thank you," he whispered, his throat clogged with tears. "This means so much."

They came around the desk to hug him and it wasn't the first time they'd done it. They were, after all, a very huggy family. But it felt different.

He had their blessing and he was grateful

Step Two was the Riverview Inn. He'd enlisted Alice to make pancakes and bacon, and when he arrived she was just finishing it up. Plating it and putting one of those silver domes over it. She'd also dipped strawberries in chocolate and put coffee in a carafe.

There was also a cold bottle of champagne.

"Alice?" he asked. "What do you think is going to happen this morning?"

"Look, Micah. Do you know how many proposals I've been a part of at this inn? Dozens. I know the look. Good luck. I'm rooting for you. Now go before my food gets cold."

"We're ah…not going to need the champagne," he said. "I don't drink and she's…"

She shook her head at him, her lips twisted in a knowing smile. She turned the bottle so he could see the label. "Sparkling juice," he read. "How…?"

She tapped the side of her head.

"Thank you," he said. "I need Bea."

"Bea!" Alice shouted, and the little girl came barreling through the kitchen's swinging door, her cousin Stella on her tail.

"How was the sleepover?" he asked her as she jumped into his arms.

"Great. We made chocolate dipped strawberries." Her mouth was covered in chocolate.

"Awesome." He gave her a squeeze and set her down. "Can you help me carry this stuff?"

"Sure!" She took the fizzy juice and he took the tray with everything else and they walked from the kitchen of the Riverview down the path to Cabin Nine.

He didn't care if they eloped or got married at the Riverview or in Madison Square Garden. He didn't care if they got married tomorrow or next year. But he was going to be her husband. And a father to Bea.

And to the baby they'd made in a bathroom backstage in Rome.

She was two months pregnant and deeply morning sick. When the tour was finishing, he'd reached out to Alice to see if there were any cabins free for them to rent, just to recuperate and relax, and she put them up in Cabin Nine. Bea had been bopping from grandparents to cousins to aunts and uncles, and he and Helen had been sleeping.

"Mom's going to love this," Bea said with total assurance.

Bea was, without a doubt, the best partner in crime a guy could have and an absolute gem of a human. He watched her, marching beside him toward the cabin, her black curls clipped back in what had to be seven sparkly barrettes.

Evan, he thought. *I'll look after her. I swear it. Your daughter will never not know love.*

Oh, fuck, he was getting a little teary. Again.

He blamed Jonah and the ring in his back pocket.

He unlocked the door to the cabin, which was dark and hushed, the curtains drawn against the sun. Helen lay in the bed, the blankets pulled up over her shoulder.

He'd played to packed arenas. Been on countless talk shows. Shaken the hand of the President.

And he'd never been so nervous.

"Oh my god," Helen groaned. "What's that smell?"

Oh no. They'd been through this before. "Good smell or bad smell?"

"Good."

He and Bea looked at each other in relief. Once at a restaurant in London someone thirty feet away from her had been eating sausage and she'd barely made it to the bathroom.

"Nope." Helen changed her mind. "Bad smell. Bacon is a bad smell."

He put the tray on the ground and lifted the dome and Bea, always ready to throw herself into danger for her family, grabbed the bacon and shoved it into her mouth.

"Good thinking," he told her.

He stepped carefully around the bed and Helen sat up, looking like the love of his life and also a little like death warmed over.

"Bea, honey?" Helen said. "I love you so much but can you take that bacon smell outside?"

Bea nodded, still chewing, and stepped out of the cabin.

"I have some options for you," he said. "Pancakes. Strawberries dipped in chocolate. Fizzy juice or coffee?"

"Pancakes sound…not terrible."

"Pancakes it is," he said with a wide smile. He set her up with the tray on the bed and then sat down on the edge.

"You're really the sweetest. I'm so sorry I'm such a mess right now."

"You are having my baby, Helen. You never have to apologize. But…" He lifted his hip and pulled out the black ring box. "I have another option for you."

"I maybe could have some coffee," she said. "Just a little. Maybe…" She saw the box and her mouth fell open.

"The option is me and you. And Bea and little Roman in your stomach there—"

"We are not calling the baby Roman."

"Fine. You can name the baby if you just say…" He opened the box. "Yes."

"Oh my god." She burst into tears. "That's my grandmother's ring."

"Jonah gave it to me."

"You talked to Jonah?"

"He says you have to marry me." She looked shocked. "I'm kidding. Your parents gave us their blessing." He kissed her messy head because she was just so incredibly dear to him.

Marry me…something something…Dear to me. Hmmm…he liked that.

"Are you writing a song in the middle of proposing to me?"

"No." He took the ring out of the box and took her hand in his. "What do you say?"

The door to the cabin opened and Bea jumped back in. "No more bacon," she said opened her mouth wide as if to prove it. She bounded up onto the bed, against Jonah's back. Her arms around his neck. "Mom, did you have the strawberries? I made them."

Helen leaned up wrapped her arms around Micah and her daughter.

"Oh mom," Bea said. "I think you are a bad smell."

Micah laughed, he couldn't help it. He laughed until the tears burned in his eyes and he held onto these girls with both hands and his whole heart.

"Yes," Helen said, blinking her green eyes at him. "I say yes. Of course, yes. Forever. Yes."

THANK YOU SO MUCH for reading Second Chance At The Riverview Inn! I hope you enjoyed Micah and Helen and the whole family as much as I did. If you have a character in this series you'd like to see more of - drop me a line! molly@molly-okeefe.com

Sign up for my newsletter!

If you'd like more emotional contemporary romance keep reading for a sneak peek of THE STORY OF US.

For ten years, Samantha Riggins and J. D. Kronos have convinced themselves they have the perfect relationship: no strings, no commitment, no future. All that changes when the son Sam gave up for adoption walks into her shelter—the son J.D. knows nothing about. The presence of their child breaks through all the rules they've lived by. And suddenly what Sam thought she knew about J.D. turns out to be wrong. Are the feelings they share enough to keep them together? Especially now that the biggest secret is the one Sam never saw coming?

———

The young ones, as a rule, were hard.

The young *pregnant* ones were heartbreaking.

Samantha Riggins watched the girl sitting in her office, clearly trying hard not to cry, and wondered how many more young pregnant girls Sam could help before jumping off the deep end.

There was a limit. There had to be.

"She hasn't said anything?" Samantha asked Deb, who'd checked in the girl while Sam taught an evening computer class.

"Nothing helpful," Deb said with a heavy sigh and arched eyebrows that reminded Sam that the young pregnant ones never said anything helpful. "Gave us the name Jane Doe and insisted she's twenty-one."

If Jane Doe was twenty-one Sam would eat her dog Daisy's dinner. "Anything else?" she asked, turning to watch Deb, who had walked in the doors of Serenity House Women's Shelter four years ago just like Jane Doe. Young. Pregnant. Terrified.

At least Jane Doe didn't appear beaten. Not like Deb had been, beaten to within an inch of dying.

"She's scared," Deb said, leaning against the kitchen counter. "But she's not talking. She's from the East Coast, maybe New York." She shook her head, her turquoise-and-rhinestone glasses catching the last of the light through the windows and tossing it around the room. "And that black hair is about as real as mine," Deb said, touching the blond tips of her long black braids. "She's got dye on her neck and hands. She's running, that girl, and she's not looking back."

Sam's worst suppositions were realized. Of course, young, pregnant women with bus-station dye jobs didn't show up at Serenity House because they'd heard the food was good.

They came because Northwoods, North Carolina, was the last stop on the southernmost tracks of a train heading out of the snarl that was New York, Newark, D.C. and Baltimore.

And they came because they were in trouble.

"For what it's worth, there's something about her that seems different," Deb said. "She's got a manicure. And a diamond ring she's wearing on a chain around her neck, that she ain't hocked yet. And them jeans she's got on cost two hundred dollars."

Sam shot Deb a dubious look. As if any of them would know two-hundred-dollar jeans if they came up and bit them in the butt.

"I read *People*," Deb explained. "They talk a lot about expensive jeans in that magazine. Can't help it if I've got an eye for fashion."

Sam smiled. Calling Deb's obsession with sequins and studding an "eye" was stretching it.

"All I'm saying is that girl is running from money," Deb said. "And that ain't ever a good thing for us."

No. It wasn't. It meant whomever this girl was running from had resources. Lawyers. Private investigators.

Luckily, Serenity House had a private investigator they could call, too, if they needed. But Sam was always careful about calling J.D.

"Thank you," she said to Deb, who, in the years since arriving and staying, had become the most valued asset Serenity House had. And not just because Deb's mother had taught her about plumbing.

"No problem," the young woman said and checked her watch. "It's eight o'clock. I need to pick up Shonny and get on home." She looked at Sam askance. "Unless you want me to stay here tonight?"

"No, thank you, Deb," Sam said, appreciating the offer. "We'll be okay."

"All right then, you want me to call J.D., get his help on this?"

The ripple that pulsed through her body was a familiar one. It happened anytime someone said his name.

"I'll call him after I talk to her," Sam said, making sure not to look at the shrewd Deb. Her secrets were under lock and key, but Deb was pretty good with locks, too.

Sam stepped into her cluttered office without looking at the girl who had gone rigid. While most people's offices were their sanctuary, Sam's was her garbage disposal. Her trash heap. Her storage closet. Her giant pounding headache. Books. Receipts. Sheets for the single beds, towels for the showers. Boxes of soap, all piled up around her desk.

And now amongst the clutter and flotsam was one thin, terrified, probably six-months-pregnant girl.

Just one more thing to wash up on her shores.

Sam made a big production of setting down her class notes, then cleaning stuff off her desk. Organizing files, throwing things out, all while watching the girl from under her eyelashes.

Oh, Jane Doe was scared. And Deb was right, the girl had cash. All the details pointed to money. She had good skin. Her face was full, as though she hadn't gone hungry a day in her life. No track marks on her arms. And, most telling, she had great teeth—sparkling white and straight. Dental hygiene, for the women who usually walked through the doors, was pretty far down the priority list.

Those teeth of Jane Doe's put Sam's instincts on full alert.

Sam had a responsibility to the rest of the women who used this shelter. While there were only two living here at the moment, they had all been brutalized in some fashion and they didn't need what this girl was running from to come hammering on the door in the wee hours of the morning.

"So," she finally said, studying her half-finished grocery list as though it was the girl's induction papers. "Jane."

The girl nodded, the flat black of her hair swallowing the light from the lamp on the desk. Dye job. All the way. "That's me," the girl said, her voice sounding as though it was dragged across sandpaper before coming out her lips.

"You want to tell me what's going on?" Sam asked. She sat back in her whiny chair and crossed her legs, careful to avoid the duct tape on the seat that snagged all of her tights. "What we can do to help you?"

"I just need a place to stay for a few nights," she said, the words tumbling out in a rush, as if she realized Sam might say no.

"We're not a hotel," Sam said. "And while I am happy to let you stay here tonight, I can only do so if you answer some questions."

"I already answered a bunch of questions," Jane said. "That other woman asked them."

"Well, I have a few more you need to answer."

"Or what?" she asked, the pale skin of her face practically vibrating, her whole body tuned to some high frequency. The edge of her Tommy Hilfiger T-shirt trembled, channeling the energy of the thin body beneath it.

"Or, perhaps you would be better helped by the police."

Jane swallowed and shook her head. "I can't go to the police."

"Why not?"

"Does it matter?" the girl asked, her blue eyes flashing. "My name is Jane. I'm twenty-one and my boyfriend hit me. I am scared for myself and my baby so you have to take me in."

Sam's eyebrows rose in surprise. "I don't, Jane. This is not a government facility. We are primarily privately funded. And as the executive director, I choose who we help and who I send on to the police. I have a responsibility to the women who live here." Not that there were that many. Jane was their only new resident in two months, but she didn't need to know that. "I have to keep them safe and if you can't tell me what I need to know, I will have to call the police."

They locked eyes, a showdown that Sam had been in and won too many times to count. But she had to give the girl credit, she was not going down without a fight.

"Jane." She sighed. "I want to help you. I spend my life helping women in your position. If you answer my questions, I can take better care of you. I am not the enemy."

Jane's lip trembled before she bit it so hard the pink skin turned white. Sam held her breath and finally exhaled when Jane looked down at her hands, the battle over.

"What do you need to know?"

"Is there someone looking for you?"

Jane's throat bobbed. "He thinks I'm visiting my sister at school."

Sam didn't point out that sisters could be called. Cover stories could be blown.

"How old are you?" she asked.

"Twenty-one."

"Jane—"

Her blue eyes blazed. "I'm twenty-one and it was consensual and I want this baby. I want—" Tears flooded those eyes, dousing the fire. "I want this baby," she whispered. "I just need a few days to think."

There was no question Jane had lied about her age, but the rest of it smelled like the truth. The truth doused with the acrid tang of fear. Whatever this girl had behind her it wasn't good.

"Have you broken the law? Is that why you're running?"

Jane's brow furrowed as if she were thinking. "No," she finally answered. "I'm pretty sure I haven't broken any laws. I didn't steal anything. I didn't hurt anyone."

"Does your family—"

"They don't know anything," she snapped. "I made sure they don't know anything. My dad would—" Jane stopped, stared hard at her hands and didn't say another word.

"Your dad would what?" Sam asked carefully, feeling the tension in the air like humidity.

"Nothing," the girl said, not looking up from her hands. "My dad's got nothing to do with this."

The hair on the back of Sam's neck didn't like that answer one bit.

"It's late." Sam took pity on the poor girl. "I can give you a room for the night, but tomorrow morning you and I are going to have a talk."

"I'm telling the truth," Jane said, defensive and stoic. "I swear to you."

And if Sam had money for every time someone swore the truth to her, she would have retired to a tropical island long ago.

"Okay." Sam nodded. "For your protection and for the protection of the other women who live here I do have to notify the police. Chief Bigham will have a patrol car out front."

Jane's chin jerked. "You won't tell them—"

"Sweetheart, I don't know anything to tell them. But if someone has filed a missing person report on you, it's only a matter of time."

"I know." Jane's shoulders bent under an unseen weight.

Sam had learned the hard way over the years that, with the young pregnant ones, the person who filed the missing person report was often the threat. Mothers or fathers so angry with their child's mistakes that they lost their minds. Or boyfriends. They could lose their minds, too.

Serenity House could help Jane until the police came looking for her. Laws protected women's shelters.

Too bad they couldn't do as much for the young pregnant girls who could use the protection. She'd seen a lot of girls beaten down by the system, chewed up and spit right back out to the people who abused them and Sam wasn't sure how much justice there was in that.

"Let's get you to bed," Sam said, unlocking the top drawer of her old metal desk and grabbing the key to room three. "Things will seem better in the morning."

She led Jane Doe of the bad hair and fancy pants, from her office right into the kitchen. Dinner had finished about an hour ago and the dishwasher chugged quietly in the evening shadows. The wooden counters, table and two high chairs were wiped clean and the smell of Deb's spaghetti lingered in the air.

"I thought a women's shelter would look different," Jane said.

"What do you mean?"

"This is like a house," the girl said, shrugging.

"I should hope so," Sam said, proud of the handsome two-story brick house with the stained-glass windows and the class-room addition built off the side. "It's my home."

"You live here?"

I rarely leave here, she thought, but only nodded.

"Is there air-conditioning?" Jane asked, pulling at the neck of her shirt. It was late June in North Carolina and the nights weren't cooling off the way they had a few weeks ago.

"Yes," she said. "We turn it off at night. Your room has a fan. Breakfast is at seven," she said. "On weekdays we serve breakfast to women and children in the community. But on the weekends it's just us. We take turns cooking and if you miss breakfast, there's nothing hot until dinner. But there's usually fruit and granola bars." Sam opened the big pantry cupboards and snagged two granola bars and handed them to Jane.

They were plucked from her hands pretty darn fast.

"The living room is through there," she said, pointing to the doorway on the far end of the kitchen. The sounds of canned laughter from the television seeped out from under the door and she knew Juny and Sue were in there watching TV. Sam would introduce Jane later; no need for everyone to get overwhelmed. "Our classrooms are on the other side of the living room. Tomorrow is Saturday so there are no classes. Though you are welcome to use the computers if you need to."

The computers had all been paid for by Sam's private benefactor two years ago. The modern age took a while to reach Serenity House but now that it was here Sam tried very hard to take care of it.

"And through here—" she turned and opened the swinging door with her butt "—are the bedrooms."

The young girl's eyes were wide, as if she'd not ever thought about the reality of shelters. The shabby cleanliness of it all. The communal reality of women coming together over hardship to make a new start.

Welcome to your new world, Sam thought.

"What kind of classes?" Jane asked, her hand tucked carefully over the small bump of her stomach.

"Computers, reading, clerical. As well as nutrition, child care—"

"Child care?"

Sam nodded, wishing just once a woman would come to this shelter armed with information. Knowledge. But they didn't and when she'd taken over the shelter ten years ago, teaching had become goal one. Not just for the women who lived in the three bedrooms, but for women in the community. They had started coming to the center for classes in droves, once the word got out.

"We've got lots of books, too," Sam said. "Have you been to a doctor?"

Sam saw the lie in the girl's eyes before it came out her mouth, but then something changed. Fear or pride or whatever it was that had put this girl on the road to Serenity House took a backseat and sense took over. "No," she said. "But I feel the baby move all the time."

"That's good," Sam said, turning around to lead Jane down

the small hallway to room three. "But we'll get you set up with a doctor tomorrow."

Jane didn't say thank-you, but Sam could feel the waves of relief that rolled over the girl.

"And here we are." Sam opened the door, revealing a small room with a single bed, table, chair and desk. All used. All well-worn. Like everything else at Serenity House. "It's not much, but it's private and clean. You've been told the rules about drugs and let me reiterate that we're very serious when it comes to prohibiting them."

"I don't do drugs," Jane said.

And where have I heard that before, Sam thought.

"Ohmigod," Jane breathed, the little color she had in her face leaching out. "Don't move."

A low growl rippled down the hall from behind Sam and she smiled, trying to reassure the terrified girl before turning. "Don't worry," she said. "That's Daisy."

"D-D-Daisy?" Jane asked, sounding dubious.

A hundred-pound Rottweiler named Daisy was admittedly ludicrous but Sam thought calling the dog Killer was a bit redundant.

"Come here, Dais," Sam said, holding out her hand to the big black beast that she loved to a stupid degree, for reasons she didn't bother to scrutinize. "Come meet your new duck."

"Duck?" Jane asked, still rattled by the dog. Jane Doe was not a dog person.

"To Daisy you are a duck," Sam said, looking over her shoulder at the girl. "And Daisy takes good care of her ducks."

Understanding dawned in Jane's eyes and she relaxed slightly. Daisy padded up to Sam and held out her nose for a good rub. Sam made the introductions and made sure Daisy got a good noseful of Jane's scent.

The last woman who hadn't met Daisy at the outset found herself pinned to the wall in the middle of the night when she'd come out to use the bathroom. Daisy had stood guard until Sam showed up and called the dog off.

Since then, meeting Daisy became part of the induction process.

"She's a good guard dog," Sam explained. "No one who she doesn't know gets in here. Between Daisy and the patrol car that will be outside you are safe tonight."

"Safe," the girl repeated. "That's good."

Sam knew the concept was foreign to a lot of the women who appeared here, but she couldn't quite get a bead on Jane. Relieved but not grateful. Tough and stubborn. Smart but not smart enough to avoid the situation she was in. She had a sister in school and she knew whoever was looking for her would contact the police. And that thing about her dad really stuck in Sam's craw.

She definitely needed to call in J.D.

Thank God.

Jane took the key from Sam's hand and stepped into her room, a thin young wisp of a girl who was practically swallowed by the shadows.

"Where is your room?" Jane asked. "I mean…will you be here?"

Sam pointed above their heads. "Upstairs," she said. "I'm here all the time."

Nodding, as if that suited her, Jane shut the door and Sam waited until she heard the lock hammer home.

Sam headed to her office to call Chief Bigham. Northwoods was a small town and, outside of a few high-school boys getting drunk and climbing the water tower every summer, Serenity House was the only thing that kept the meager police force busy.

Well, that and the drugs that filtered down from the city on the very highway and train tracks that brought the women searching for Serenity.

But the chief was looking at retirement next year and he didn't do too much about the drugs. And the few times Sam had called looking for some information or help, he'd been less than helpful.

Didn't like to get involved in domestic situations, he said.

"Well, good evening, Samantha," Chief said, after picking up the phone. "What can I do for you tonight?"

"I've got a Jane Doe, Chief."

"You want me to check the computer?"

"No." She knew that him checking the computer was about as helpful as him looking up in the stars for information. "We're calling in our guy on this. I don't want to take up your resources with what might be a wild-goose chase."

Sam figured that if she called J.D. tonight, unless he was already involved in a case, it wouldn't take him too long to get here.

A day. Two.

Jane needed a few days of rest. A chance to see a doctor, get her bearings before Sam dug for more information. She said she hadn't broken any laws and Sam believed her but there was still more to her story. Usually after a night of sleep followed by a good breakfast, the silent girls tended to open up like coin purses.

"I could use some men out front, just in case," she said. It had taken Chief Bigham a while to come around to even the idea of having a car out front when a new woman came to the shelter. But having a homicidal husband track down his family to the shelter —with fatal results—had convinced the chief of the necessity for added protection.

"No problem, Sam. I'll send Paul."

Sam smiled. Paul and Daisy went way back, so the dog should mind her manners. "Thanks, Chief," she said and hung up.

She set the cell phone down on the desk, right in the pool of light cast by the lamp.

Now, she thought, staring at the phone. What to say to J.D.?

I need your help. Oh, and Bob and I broke up. I miss you so much my whole body hurts.

Shaking her head at her own folly, she dialed the number she knew by heart even though she only called him a few times a year.

"J.D.," his strong voice said. "Leave a message."

Sam took a deep breath while the phone beeped. "Hi, J.D., it's me. Sam. We've got a little situation down here and I could use your expertise. Feel free to call me back on my cell. Anytime." *Don't do it. Control yourself, woman.* "Oh, and Bob and I broke up. That's—" *Idiot!* "Yeah, that's all. Talk to you soon."

She disconnected the phone and tossed it on the desk, disgusted with herself and, stupidly, alive with a little thrill.

J.D. was coming to town.

* * *

It took an hour for Sam to complete her nightly walkthrough. She was worried about the pipes in the kitchen—the slow leak was becoming more than Deb could fix. And Sam's maintenance budget was down to zero thanks to the last storm that sent a tree through the roof of one of the classrooms.

So she changed the pan under the leak and hoped it would hold until she could discuss budgets with her bookkeeper and determine if she was going to have to call her benefactor.

Glancing out the window over the sink, she saw the patrol car pull up in front of the old oak tree. Paul flashed his lights once, without the siren, then killed the engine.

No moon tonight. No stars.

The dim lights from town shone beyond the trees to the west. Other than that, it was nothing but southern black sky, as far as the eye could see.

Sam wasn't scared of much, and the dark wasn't on the list. But those things that lived in the dark, that threatened her shelter and the women therein, were terrifying.

Made a woman glad to have a hundred-pound killer dog on the premises.

As if reading her mind, Daisy stepped to her side as Sam entered the living room, only to find Juny and her fourteen-year-old daughter, Sue, asleep on the couch in front of the flickering TV.

Curled up like kittens.

She was reluctant to wake the two—both of them slept better with lights on and white noise. But rules were rules. These two women had been their only residents for four months. Sam knew she should have been urging them to move on sooner, but frankly, with so few women staying here these days, Sam felt lonely in the big house. As it was, Juny had gotten a job and the two of them would be leaving bright and early in the morning. Moving out.

Sam smiled, looking at them. Another success story for Serenity.

She sent them, rubbing their eyes, to their bedrooms, and turned off the TV. The darkness followed her through the house, a black cat constantly in her path.

Daisy stayed on the main floor and Sam unlocked her door and climbed the stairs to her rooms on the second floor.

If her office was her headache, her bedroom, kitchen, living room and giant bathroom were her sanctuary. Her grandmother's furniture filled the four rooms she called home, and since her grandmother had had cash and taste, the rooms looked excellent.

She sighed, letting Jane Doe and the pipes slide right off her back along with the white scooped-neck shirt she wore. It puddled on the floor in front of her white-and-red twill couch and she kicked off her red flats by the oak coffee table.

In the doorway of her kitchen she pulled out the pins that held her red hair in a knot and dropped them in her grandmother's cabbage-leaf teacup that was filled with pins and pennies.

Like Daisy after a nap, she gave herself a good hard shake.

Thinking of a hot bath, a cold beer and the possibility of J.D.'s voice in her ear by the end of the night, she unzipped her black skirt and peeled off her tights—noting, with a curse, that the chair with the duct tape had taken a bite out of another pair of black tights.

Wearing just her white bra and pink polka-dotted underwear, she pushed open the door to her deliciously pink, unrepentantly feminine bathroom. Steam spilled out over her feet. Misting over her legs.

"What—"

Her tub was full. Bubbles, a foamy frothy delight of them, spilled over the lip of her claw-foot tub. The scent of roses was in the hot, humid air.

And sitting, a bit of the dark night condensed, a thrilling spot of masculinity on the closed lid of her toilet, smiling like a man with a secret, was J.D.

Want More? THE STORY OF US

www.ingramcontent.com/pod-product-compliance
Lightning Source LLC
Chambersburg PA
CBHW071309140726
47996CB00005B/1692